T0277341

Finding Home

A Windrush Story

Alford Dalrymple Gardner
and
Howard Gardner

JACARANDA

This edition first published in Great Britain 2023
Jacaranda Books Art Music Ltd
27 Old Gloucester Street,
London WC1N 3AX
www.jacarandabooksartmusic.co.uk

A CIP catalogue record for this book is available from the British Library

ISBN: 9781914344220
eISBN: 9781914344213

Cover design: Rodney Dive
Typeset: Kamillah Brandes

For Norma and Jean
—Alford

For my wife Helen
—Howard

Foreword

THE MEMOIR OF ALFORD DALRYMPLE GARDNER
A Jamaican Windrush Story
2023

Alford Dalrymple Gardner was among the passengers on MV *Empire Windrush* which arrived at Tilbury Docks, Essex, England, on 22 June 1948, and it is because of this ship that he has become known nationally and internationally.

On Wednesday June 23, 1948, *The Times* newspaper reported the arrival of the ship under the headline 'Jamaicans Arrive to Seek Work'. The article said: 'Of the 492 Jamaicans who arrived at Tilbury on Monday to seek work in this country, 236 were housed last night in Clapham South Deep Shelter. The remainder had friends to whom they could go and prospects of work. The men had arrived at Tilbury in the ex-troopship *Empire Windrush*. Among them are singers, students, pianists, boxers, and a complete dance band. Thirty or forty had already volunteered to work as miners.'

The report was not entirely correct. According to the ship's Passenger List there were 1027 passengers on board, of whom 539 gave Jamaica as their last place of permanent residence, so did 139 from Bermuda, 73 from Trinidad and 44 from British Guiana. Many others came from countries of the West Indies. Some of them served Britain in the Royal Air Force (RAF) during WWII and were either returning to their jobs in the UK or coming to seek employment. For the passengers of the *Empire Windrush* in 1948, and the thousands who followed them, the British Nationality Act Parliament passed in July 1948 was an important factor, as it allowed them and others living in Commonwealth countries British citizenship and full rights of entry and settlement. The Nationality Bill was being discussed in both Houses of Parliament even as the ship sailed across the Atlantic to Britain during June 1948.

MV *Empire Windrush* which brought passengers to Britain was once known as the *Monte Rosa*, a passenger liner and a cruise ship launched in Germany in 1930. During WWII, the Germans used her as a troop-ship, but after the war she was taken by the British, renamed MV *Empire Windrush* and became a troopship until March 1954, when she caught fire and sank in the Mediterranean Sea. The ship was said to have been named after the 'River Windrush' which begins in the Cotswold Hills in Gloucestershire. MV *Empire Windrush* was the opportunity that hundreds of young Caribbean men, like Alford, awaited in 1948.

On board the ship, Alford met Samuel Beaver King, another former RAF serviceman, also age 22, who shared the same ideals and who looked forward to leading a new life in Britain. King included Alford's name among dozens of others in his address book. They kept in touch over the years and in 1998, King brought together many of the *Windrush* passengers to commemorate the 40th anniversary of the ship's 22 June 1948 arrival. Alford joined local celebrations in Leeds in June 2008 and contributed to a Windrush Foundation oral history project which recorded *Empire Windrush* stories. It was in that year that I first met and interviewed Alford.

I am co-founder, with Samuel Beaver King, of Windrush Foundation, an organisation that became a charity in 1996 to keep alive the memories of the ship's arrival and to commemorate Windrush Day annually on 22 June. The 50th anniversary celebrations were featured on British media, and many events were held including a Reception hosted by HRH Prince Charles at St James's Palace in June 1998.

It is due to the *Empire Windrush* that I have come to know Alford, a pioneering member of the Windrush generation. He is among those who helped to rebuild Britain after World War Two, and who laid the foundation in Britain for thousands of settlers from the Caribbean. The ship has a symbolic association with Caribbean settlement from 22 June 1948, but it also represents a generation of WWII West Indian ex-service personnel who remained in the UK just after May 1945.

There are no published or official figures for those who served, either as servicemen and women, or munition workers. They had contributed to the war effort either as volunteers in the armed forces or as technicians. The majority were demobbed and returned to the colonies. Before leaving the armed forces, West Indian servicemen and women were given opportunities to attend educational and technical courses that often lasted between six months and two years. Sponsored by the Colonial Office, they were known as rehabilitation courses. Some personnel studied to become engineers, farmers, carpenters, accountants, lawyers or pursue other skills. Covert attempts were made to pressurise them to return to their own colonies although all the ex-service personnel were British subjects and had the right to remain. An ex-serviceman who experienced coercion explained:

> 'When my course ended, I wanted to stay in England to acquire further qualifications, but the colonial office did their best to dissuade me. They kept telling me: "Well you can't stay here you must go back and help your own people, after all you did sign to stay for the duration of the present emergency," and this and that. However when they saw I was adamant, particularly when I pointed out that I was a British subject, I was entitled to domicile in the UK and they couldn't legally send me home, they desisted from further pressuring, so I stayed.'[1]

There were thousands of UK job vacancies in 1947, yet West Indian ex-servicemen continued to experience difficulties obtaining suitable work, mainly because of their 'skin colour'. Ex-serviceman Robert N.

Murray, in his 1996 book, *Lest We Forget* discusses his colleague, Pasteur Irons's hunt for work:

'...being married with children I was desperate for work. I went for a job at one ironworks. I passed the test, tried everything but they turned me down. Then I went to another well-known company. They told me to wait while they interviewed all the ex-prisoners of war, the very people we left our homelands to fight against. It was then more than anytime I regretted staying in England, for nothing could be more humiliating than my early job-seeking experiences. Footslogging looking for jobs everyday became tedious and depressing. I sometimes became scared; scared not of people, but of being rejected and of my aggressive retaliation. But what could I do? I had to carry on, I dare not lose hope...'[2]

The Spring of 1947 saw the arrival, at Liverpool Docks, of the troop-ship SS *Ormonde*, with 108 passengers, most of whom were West Indian ex-servicemen, and there were 10 stowaways on board. Labour members of Parliament who were in power at the time openly expressed their unhappiness about the settlers' arrival. In December that year, the HMS *Almanzora* landed with 150 West Indian ex-servicemen also among the passengers. WWII RAF serviceman Samuel Beaver King had been one of the passengers of the *Almanzora* as it took British troops and ex-servicemen to Jamaica in November 1947. He was demobbed like thousands of other West Indian men and women who had served Britain during WWII.

After MV *Empire Windrush* landed on 22 June 1948, her passengers disembarked, and those who had nowhere to stay were accommodated at Clapham South Deep Shelter, London, which had been an air-raid shelter for local people during WWII. Within a few days, the Mayor of Lambeth held a reception for them, and this was the only one they received. The passengers visited the local employment exchange in Brixton and soon found work, and many set up home in the borough.

Alford headed for Leeds after disembarking on the ship. His book discusses the problems he and others faced in their search for accommodation, employment, and other pursuits.

2018 was the 70th Windrush anniversary and it brought to light injustices suffered by thousands of Caribbean men and women in the UK. They were wrongly classified as illegal immigrants by the Home Office and were cut from access to any public services including health care. Also, the British government made working or renting accommodation without adequate paperwork impossible for them. The government's 'hostile environment' prevented their visiting doctors for fear of amassing huge bills or being deported. It prevented undocumented immigrants from reporting crime to the police. It deterred undocumented migrants from reporting unsafe working conditions or exploitative employers. It reduced the options for renting a home and pushed people into poor quality accommodation.

Hostile environment policies also made doctors, landlords, teachers, and other public sector workers responsible for immigration checks. The situation came to a head when the British media in March 2018 exposed and labelled it the 'Windrush scandal', blaming the government for the desperate circumstances in which the people, who had the right to be in the UK, found themselves. The 'Windrush generation' became a media term for a tragedy in government policy that destroyed the lives of hundreds of British citizens from the Caribbean. Many of them have died after receiving government apologies after April 2018 and without receiving the compensation that the Home Office promised would be given speedily.

The 'Windrush generation' is a term first coined by Samuel Beaver King after his arrival on the ship *Empire Windrush* on 22 June 1948. In 1996, King and Torrington created a registered charity that commemorated the ship's arrival, celebrated 22 June as Windrush Day, and organised activities that celebrated the men and women who settled in Britain after WWII. King was the one who first brought together in 1988 dozens of fellow passengers to commemorate the June 1948 arrival. There had been none in the 1950s. Donald Hind's 1966 book *Journey to an Illusion* (page 52-53) refers to the ship but briefly included only two stories about the passengers. Most noteworthy is an interview with a WWII RAF ex-serviceman who told him, 'that was the time that the *Empire Windrush* became a household word in the West Indies as ex-servicemen and their relatives trekked north. After a while people started writing to us, asking us to meet their relations and see that they received some sort of accommodation.'

Windrush stories were not a topic of conversation during the 1950s. There were dozens of other ships taking West Indian settlers to the UK at the time, until the 1960 when the trek was via British Overseas Airways Corporation (BOAC). King and Torrington's Windrush Foundation built the platform upon which all other organisations that use the word 'Windrush' stand. The Foundation was the major organiser of national commemorative events from 1996 to date.

The book you are reading is about a pioneering member of the Windrush generation. His life and experiences will inspire you, as it is one of courage, adventure, tenacity, survival, humour, and you would have your own words to describe him. Volunteering for the Royal Air Force was a major decision giant leap forward, and like his father had done before him as a volunteer in the First World War and survived. Their contributions to Britain have been inestimable.

I will say no more and let you get on with reading this book!
ENJOY!

—Arthur Torrington CBE
Co-founder, and Director of Windrush Foundation, 2023

The British in Jamaica

B efore I get to my story, I would like to give you a little bit of history about the beautiful island of my birth.[1]

In 1494, Christopher Columbus came across the island now known as Jamaica. The island was inhabited by the indigenous people known as Taíno. With the arrival of the Spanish, a large proportion of the Taíno people died from diseases imported from Europe. The Spanish enslaved the Taíno people, but as so many Taínos died the Spanish started to bring in slaves from Africa.

In the mid-1600s both freed African slaves and African slaves who had escaped from plantations, moved into the mountain regions of the island. They called themselves Maroons. Some of the remaining Taínos also moved into the mountains and integrated with the Maroons. When war broke out with the British in 1654, the Maroons and surviving Taínos joined forces with the Spanish, even when the Spanish were eventually defeated and the British took over the island the Maroons continued the fight against the British, right up to the emancipation of slavery.[2]

In 1654, Oliver Cromwell, ordered his armed forces to attack San Domingo which was the largest Spanish island in the West Indies. Today, it is divided politically into the Republic of Haiti (in the west) and the Dominican Republic (in the east). The English expedition left England that year and was led by Admiral Sir William Penn and General Robert Venables with a fleet of warships and transports, carrying cannons, and soldiers. The fleet first sailed to Barbados where reinforcement was sought from other English West Indian colonies. They were joined by Leeward Island volunteers which included soldiers, planters, and their enslaved Africans.

The invaders landed on the Spanish colony, but many soon afterwards suffered from the effects of tropical diseases. Their attack on the Spaniards was a disaster and the English abandoned further attempts to capture the island after losing hundreds of men. The English decided to salvage something from the expedition by attacking and capturing the smaller island of Jamaica, which was poorly defended by the Spaniards.

Cromwell was not happy after he had heard what had happened in the West Indies. However, he took action to preserve and improve Jamaica, the new colony. The Spanish were expelled, a task that the English accomplished within five years.

The British built a base at Port Royal, where, among other activities, piracy flourished, attracting national rebels who had been ejected from their countries to serve their sentences on the high seas. One of the most notorious was Captain Henry Morgan, a plantation owner and privateer. A pressing need for constant defence of the island against Spanish reprisals was removed when England obtained ownership of the island from Spain in 1670 through the Treaty of Madrid. Jamaica's population dramatically increased after Cromwell sent indentured servants and prisoners to the island and the new settlers included thousands of Irish men and women.

The British military governor in Jamaica, always fearful of Spanish reprisals (despite the treaty), sought the support of buccaneers who moved to Port Rush. The port had become well known for its wealth and lawlessness. The buccaneers repeatedly attacked Spanish Caribbean territories and commerce, diverting Spanish resources, and threatening her lucrative gold and silver trade. Many buccaneers held royal commissions as privateers but remain pirates and are also freelance merchants.

In spite of tropical diseases European numbers increased, and the island's population grew from a few thousand in the mid-17th century to about 18,000 by the 1680s, with enslaved Africans said to account for more than half the total. Diseases on the island kept the number of Europeans under 30,000 during the 18th century, but the number of enslaved Africans increased to over 300,000 by 1800. Jamaica was Britain's richest overseas possession until the island gained its independence in 1962.

Today, Jamaica's population is just under three million, made up mainly of people of African descent, but also descendants of people from India and China. There are, perhaps, as many who have settled in other countries of the world over the decades. Many of those who have left the island have emigrated to the UK, USA, and Canada for economic reasons.

Hence the Jamaican motto, OUT OF MANY ONE PEOPLE.

Chapter One

M y name is Alford Dalrymple Gardner. I was born 27 January 1926 in Kingston, the capital city of Jamaica. The fourth child of eleven, I had seven sisters and three brothers. My siblings in order of birth: Minerva (Sista Nerva), Essmedora (Enez), Gladstone, myself, George, Eslyn (Lynn), Bridget (Bee), Florence (Grace), Hannah (Mate), Pamela (Mell), Samuel (GG).

My father was Egbert Watson Gardner and my mother was Lovenia Gardner. They got married in 1930, four years after my birth. At the time it was fairly common for couples to have children and then get married. Now in Jamaica there is the expectation to be married and then have children.

During WWI my father volunteered to join the army: the British West Indies Regiment (BWIR). He trained at Salisbury and saw action at the Battle of the Somme and at Ypres, but that's all I know. He never spoke about his time in the army. My father was a stoic man.

However, when I was born, he was a veteran and a policeman. A man is many things, but I think 'policeman' sums up my father. That's how the community saw him and how he interacted with them. He was well respected as a policeman, and the local people saw him as his children did, a strict but fair disciplinarian. He didn't stand for nonsense and wouldn't let you get away with anything.

Before becoming a policeman, he worked as a tailor. I know that he went to work in Cuba for about nine months, but unfortunately, I don't know what he did there; this was years before my birth. At that time it was very common for men from different islands to travel around to find work if there was nothing available locally.

Papa never spoke much about his time in the BWIR, he only said that he did his training on Salisbury Plain before moving over to Europe. Physically and mentally he was fine and on returning to Jamaica he went straight back to his job as a policeman. My research tells me that the men of the BWIR were mainly used as stretcher bearers and as helpers to build roads and gun emplacements and dig trenches. Basically, they were used as general labourers and most of the time they served within range of German artillery and snipers.

My papa was an athlete. When not on duty he would be out running or taking part in various athletic events on a weekend, often 100-metre and 200-metre events. He was so fast that he could have been in the Olympics. His best times were under the qualifying times for the Olympics, he could have gone in 1936, but he was too old by then. If only he'd trained for it and tried in his prime. Beyond the track, he liked to play tennis and just generally loved to be outside, even just walking in the countryside. Our neighbours were always saying that they had seen Papa out and about.

As for my mama, she was a very clever woman. She didn't have much of a traditional education, nor did she have any formal medical training, but she was like the local nurse. People in the village would come to her with their ailments. The neighbours trusted her, and she would always try to help them, she never turned anyone away and never charged anyone.

My mother's knowledge was that which is passed down from generation to generation combined with what she gleaned from experience. During the days of slavery, medical assistance for some of the enslaved was non-existent. The women and men had to learn how to repair cuts, bandage wounds and cool down fevers. Women like my mother have always been important to communities where medical professionals are not readily available.

One of the things that Mama would do to help her with her nursing skills, and I know that it was not a nice thing to do, but she would operate on one of our chickens. I suppose it helped if she ever had to put some stitches in a large wound.

Both my parents served our community in their own way and commanded tremendous respect from the community and their children. In another life I would have liked to be a doctor. I wonder how much of that desire came from watching my mother help everyone who came to her.

As well as being the local nurse, my mother was a housewife, she was an excellent cook. We had our own chickens and a vegetable patch, so we always had fresh meat, along with homegrown veg like yams and gungo peas. I have such fond memories of Mama's gungo pea soup, it was one of the nicest things I would eat.

Mama made clothes for all us children, but Papa would make my trousers. For some reason he never made me a pair of long trousers, even when I got older, whilst my mama would make my shirts.

Every year my father imported fashion magazines from a company in Liverpool. *Vogue, Weldon's Ladies Journal* and a few others. These magazines had free dress patterns included and within a few weeks of receiving the magazines, my sisters would be wearing the latest fashion items thanks to Mama's sewing skills. How he got to know about these magazines I don't know. Perhaps he found out about them when he was stationed in the UK. My papa was always resourceful.

I was part of a large family with seventeen years between the oldest and the youngest. Unfortunately many have passed away, only my sister Mel and my brother Sam (or GG as he is known) are still with us.

My sister Minerva (1921-?) trained to be a nurse and went to work in Trinidad once she had passed her exams. After a few years in Trinidad she moved to Cleveland, Ohio, where she married and had a family.

Essmedora, or Enez (1924-2011) as we knew her, is my half-sister. She was born in Cuba and only came to live in Jamaica when she was about seven. She lived with us for about six months, until her mother came to the island permanently, and they went to live in Montego Bay.

Gladstone, (1924-2006) was also a product of Papa's wandering eye and is my half-brother. Upon leaving school, Gladstone became an apprentice cabinetmaker, Mama seemed to accept the situation regarding Papa's infidelities and helped to look after Papa's other children as they were growing up. Gladstone moved back to Jamaica in August 1995. Gladstone and his mother, Auntie May, lived in Hopewell.

Then there was me. After me another boy, George, was born, but unfortunately passed away in infancy.

Lynn (1930-2022) comes next, when she moved to Cleveland she married an American serviceman who was stationed in Germany. They came over to see me once in the UK, that would have been about 1974. She trained as a radiographer.

Bridget, or Bee (1931-2018) to her siblings, moved to New York. She worked as a care worker and was a good dressmaker like her mother. She came to visit me in 1992. I think it was her first visit to the UK.

Florence, or Grace, (1934-2002) became a teacher and eventually a headmistress. She helped to coach the Jamaican national netball team. When she came to London with the team, I met up with her, and the first thing she wanted to do was to go to Harrods.

Hannah, or Mate, (1935-2016) also lived in New York. I have no idea what she did for a living.

Pamela, or Mel, was a care worker and is still living in New York. She came to visit me in 2018. It was her first time in the UK.

Samuel (1938), or GG, when he lived in Jamaica he worked as a distributor delivering things like cookers and TVs. He now lives in Maryland. He worked with his nephew in Cleveland, but never trained in any particular industry, he was a jack of all trades.

I love all of my siblings, but due to the age gap I never got to know some of them. Naturally I was closest to my siblings who were only a few years older or younger than me, especially Gladstone. We would cause mischief together, but not too much, as my parents were very strict, especially my father. I was always being told, 'no you can't do that.' Whatever they said, they meant it. If I didn't do what I was told there would be a beating.

We always had chores to do, one of my jobs was to keep the yard clean, the yard was not much bigger than the average living room, but if there was even one breadfruit tree leaf or any other leaf left on the ground I would be in for a licking.

I was a bright boy growing up, if I do say so myself, and I could do anything a boy could do swim, cycle, ride a horse, etc. As a family we were fortunate that my father had a good job. My brothers and sisters were always well dressed when some of my friends were walking around barefooted and wearing rags.

At the age of four the family moved from Kingston to Cambridge in the St James area of Jamaica, when my papa had a new posting. We weren't the wealthiest family, but my parents were still able to employ a couple of servants: a boy to help Papa with his horse, that was until I was old enough to help in looking after the horse and a girl to help Mama with the washing and the younger children.

One young girl who had worked with Mama for about five years, Gertie, enjoyed working for Mama so much that she did not want to stop working for Mama when we moved from Cambridge to Springfield. It was about seven miles to Springfield, so she would walk or get a lift from her house in Cambridge to our house. She would turn up on a Monday, stay a few days then walk home. Over the years there were a few girls who worked for Mama, and she liked to treat them all like daughters.

I went to school earlier than most Jamaicans, starting at four years old, it was about then that I learnt how to read and write. My school, the Montego Bay Barracks school, was considered a good school and I went there for four years. Mama took me to school for the first three weeks, showing me the way, it wasn't far.

Then Gladstone came to live with us and it would just be me and Gladstone, walking to school, holding hands the whole way. There wasn't much traffic in Jamaica then, not many cars at all, so there wasn't anything to worry about.

We moved into a house in Cambridge which was a mile from the police station. I was eight years old and my first day at Cambridge Elementary School did not go well. The standard of education in this new school was not as good as my old school in Montego Bay. My time there put me far ahead of my new classmates, some of whom were just starting school. In Cambridge, most children did not start until they were seven.

On my first day at Cambridge Elementary, the teacher wrote an exercise on the blackboard for the pupils to copy into their books. I was able to copy everything into my book very quickly, so I decided to have a little rest. I folded my arms and placed them on the desk, then put my head down on my arms, so it must have looked as if I was dozing off. I started to sing the latest song of the day to myself. I thought that I was singing the song in my head.

The teacher looked up and saw me. Enraged at seeing a boy relaxing in class, she scrambled to grab the ruler on my desk and gave me a knock on the head. I went into a rage shouting and carrying on with the teacher. The headmaster, Mr Blake, was summoned. The teacher accused me of being lazy, not realising that I had already finished the work.

Once everyone had calmed down and my work had been checked the headmaster moved me on to the next class. I was proud to move up and I still found the work quite easy, so three days later I was moved into the next grade up. Within ten days I moved up again.

The school curriculum was based on the UK system's three Rs: reading, writing and arithmetic. We also had to do Latin and even after all this time I can still say a bit, just don't ask me what it means.

From the ages of eight to twelve, I had a fight almost every day, sometimes because other students had a problem with me, but mostly because I was protecting my brother or sisters. I thought it was my duty to help them, nobody touched them if I was about. This amount of fighting might seem strange, it wasn't normal then in Jamaica either. If these fights had been my fault, I'd have been in for a whooping from my papa. I didn't seek these fights out, trouble just seemed to follow me at that age.

The first time I got into a fight was to do with my half-brother Gladstone, I was six at the time. A boy had pushed Gladstone down some steps. Someone came and told me what had happened, and when I got there Gladstone was at the bottom of the steps in tears. The boy who pushed him was the school bully, but that didn't bother me. As I rounded the corner the boy looked at me and said, 'what are you going to do?' Now in that situation, even at that age, I don't ask or answer questions. I punched the boy in the face, to show him what I was going to do. He left Gladstone alone after that.

Another incident involved my younger sister Lynn. When we left school, we had to cross over a railway line to get home. As Lynn was crossing the tracks, I was a few metres behind, chatting with my friend. A boy called Aubrey tripped her up. She fell in the middle of the tracks, hurt herself, and started to cry. I ran to them, Lynn bawling on the ground, Aubrey standing over her, laughing like it was the funniest thing in the world.

I punched him twice in the face before he even knew what hit him. I made the boy's mouth bleed, and he ran off home. We had to pass the boy's house on our way home, and we heard raised voices. 'What happened to your mouth, buoy?' his grandfather asked him.

Aubrey, now clearly crying himself, said through tears, 'it was that Gardner boy,' neglecting to mention why I had done so. His attempt to play the victim backfired though, the next thing we heard was two smacks, loud as gunshots. My punches were nothing compared to the beating Aubrey's grandfather gave him.

'You let that little buoy get the better of you?' he said in between smacking his grandson, who at this point was howling from the pain and humiliation. Aubrey tried to explain himself further as we walked out of earshot, but I don't think his grandpa was listening.

In the most significant incident, I didn't get a hit in. When I was eight, I was helping a younger boy with his ABCs and reading. This boy had an older brother, only two years older than me, but he took exception to me helping his younger brother. The little boy tried to warn me that his brother was going to beat me up for helping him. For some reason he thought that me being young myself, I shouldn't be teaching his younger brother. I ignored the threat.

The next day I was playing in the playground. It was a hot, Jamaican day and I went over to get a drink from the water tank. As I bent down to cup the water in my hand, I felt a bang on the back of my head. All I could see was stars, my vision was going black and as I was fading all I could hear was a voice shouting, 'me going to kill you.'

The boy had taken a cast iron leg from a chair and smashed me around the head with it. The next thing I remember is sitting in the head-master's office having a plaster and bandage put on my head. Thankfully there were other pupils at the water tank, they managed to stop the boy from hitting me again.

The boy was suspended from school for a few weeks, on his return to school we were brought together. The headmaster warned us that if there was any more trouble between us there would be serious consequences. I never spoke to the boy again, but I still have the indentation and the scar on the back of my head to remind me of him. Thankfully because he was young, he didn't have enough strength to hit me with too much force, or things could have been so much worse.

When not at school and after having done all my chores, I spent my time with my friends, Alan, Sidney and Dennis. There were a few more lads we hung around with, but we four were always there, insepa-rable. Once we had done all our chores, we all did what young boys do.

We played cricket, ran everywhere, rode bikes, and swam in the warm Caribbean sea and the Great River. Papa always told us to treat the river water like sea water and not drink a drop.

I didn't realise at the time what he meant, but I followed Papa's advice unquestioningly. Though the water was always clear, waste from the sewers, factories and plantations would drain off into the river. That was the best advice Papa gave me.

We were out in nature a lot as kids. Some of our neighbours had horses or mules and it was on these animals that I learnt to ride. My best friend Dennis lived just down the road from me. His parents had a cow, and I would go to meet Dennis in the early mornings to help him milk the cow. The taste of fresh milk in the morning was wonderful.

A few people had small holdings in Longridge, a place not too far from Cambridge, growing all manner of fruit and vegetables, but the bananas were our favourite. As boys we would go and help them farm. When I was twelve a developer purchased the land, and everyone had to move out. The fruit trees were left at the mercy of the animals and birds and also a group of hungry young boys. You could always tell which the best fruit was to pick first, because the birds would be eating them. Every Friday we would wait until they ripened, pick them and go cook them.

At this time I did not get to see much of my brother Gladstone; he is really my half-brother, and he lived with his mother in Hopewell. I didn't really understand or care about the implications of my father having a child with someone other than his wife, it was just how it was. My mother seemed to bear no ill-will to Gladstone, my father, or the situation, but maybe at twelve I wasn't able to see what was right in front of me.

During the school holidays I would travel to Hopewell and stay with my grandmother. I would never go hungry in Hopewell; I would go to Gladstone's and be given something to eat, then go to my grandmother's house and be given more food. As you can tell I enjoy my food, and if not for the fact that I was always on the go, running, walking, or cycling, I think that I would have been quite a big lad.

As I got older, taking care of Lucky Boy, my father's horse, became my responsibility. Papa kept Lucky Boy in a field three miles from the family home. I would go down there to feed and water the horse, and make sure he was well-groomed. Sometimes I was told to bring the horse back to the house. My father forbade me from riding the horse, it was too big and fast for a small lad, but boys will be boys and I constantly rode that horse.

One day the horse nearly demolished a house. I was leading the horse to the house when I got distracted. I tied the rope to a post and went to talk to my friend who had called me over to where he stood. I was not away long, but as I was walking back to the horse, something spooked the animal. Lucky Boy reared up.

Unknown to me, the post I had tied the horse to was attached to a veranda of a house. Luckily, I had not tied the rope too tightly otherwise the horse could have caused quite a bit of damage to the house. To avoid a beating from my parents I never mentioned the incident to them.

I had a soft spot for Lucky Boy, he was a retired racehorse and always looking to gallop, but my father wouldn't let him. To me, Papa was not a good rider. You could always hear Lucky Boy coming along the street when Papa was riding him, clip clop, clip clop. We did not have a saddle; we would just throw a blanket over it and use a rope and halter to control him.

No one ever taught me to ride; as I said, I was forbidden. So I learnt by doing. I would mount the beast and immediately he was off. Because I was small, I was able to crouch on him like a proper jockey, and just hang on for dear life.

One day Lucky Boy decided to set off at a gallop and I lost control of him. I was shouting for him to stop, pulling on the rope with all my might, all to no avail. Luckily some men working in a field noticed my struggle. One of them stepped out into the road and waved his arms around. The horse came to a halt in front of him. I jumped off the horse and from that day forward, whenever I looked at the horse, I could swear that it was smirking at me. As if to say, 'I had you worried that day.'

14

One Sunday, Papa came to me and told me not to go to church, I had to go get the horse and bring it back to the house, as he had to leave early the next morning. When I arrived at the field, Lucky Boy was at the far end of the field, but the field was full of cows. I knew that cows could be very nasty, especially if there are calves in the field. So, I called his name, hoping he would come to me. Lucky Boy and the cows turned round to look at the silly boy shouting his head off, but neither horse nor cow came to me.

After about half an hour of calling for Lucky Boy, I was getting desperate, Papa would be wondering where I was. There was a mango tree on the edge of the field. I climbed the tree and picked some mangoes, hoping to entice the beast, but he seemed content eating grass at the far end of the field. As my voice began to get hoarse from shouting louder and louder for Lucky Boy, he began to slowly walk over to me, and I was able to take him to the house.

My memories of horsing around with Lucky Boy are some of my fondest, but I enjoyed my time at school too. The great educators are the ones who inspire and encourage you. Every child should have a teacher like that and for me it was my headmaster, Mr J W Kentish. Kentish was a maths genius; he was always getting work sent up from Kingston University to work on.

He came to see my parents because he could see that I had potential to go far. I had mentioned to him that I wanted to train to become a doctor, and he urged my parents to send me to high school. Unfortunately, my parents already had two of my sisters at high school, Minerva and Enez, and with Gladstone being the older son, he would be the first in line to go to high school. In the end, Gladstone never went to high school, but it still wasn't financially possible for me to go. I was bright, so who knows where I could have ended up academically?

I didn't resent the decision though, I never expected to go to high school and it wasn't as important then as it is now. Out of curiosity I asked Papa why he would pay for the girls to go to high school but not for me or Gladstone. He said that uneducated men had more chance of employment than uneducated women and he wanted to make sure that his daughters had the education needed to find good jobs once they had left school.

I enjoyed school and because of the work I produced the teachers often used my work as an example of how the work should be done. It was a big school, split into three parts: infants, juniors, and senior school. The classes were mixed with about 20-30 pupils each. There was a strict regime in place. You had to always be on time.

Anyone stepping out of line or misbehaving would expect to get six of the best with the cane. If you went home and told your parents that you had been disciplined at school, you would get six more from them. For me the threat of a beating was the best cure to motivate a child. It was common then and my parents' discipline meant I was used to it, but I don't recall ever getting caned at school.

The only trouble I really had was fights and by then I'd grown out of fighting. The fights were out of necessity and duty, to protect my younger siblings, but after so many fights I think it had been made clear there would be consequences if anyone touched my siblings.

My last fight at school, indeed the last time I would fight anyone in Jamaica, was when I was thirteen. I don't remember how this one started, but I'm sure I didn't start it because this boy was huge. Bigger, older, and stronger than me, I definitely would have left him alone if I could have. But sometimes these things are unavoidable. So, punches flew. I was good with my fists, but he managed to take me down and my fists were useless with this brute on top of me.

I was thrashing around, doing my best to get up while avoiding a beating, but it was useless. There was a crash then a shout, 'come off o' mi brother,' and the boy fell off of me. My sister, Enez, had come to my rescue and hit the boy over the head with a rock. We each got suspended for three weeks, I think due to how bad it all looked; it took a while for his head to stop bleeding.

Other than the fighting, I was a good boy. Well-behaved, polite, and god-fearing, I put this down to my parents. I was well-raised and had a healthy fear of my father. He would cane us when we got out of line. In my early teens as I was walking home, I saw some men in a shop playing dominos, despite gambling being illegal at the time. Curiosity got the better of me and I lingered at the shop window, observing their game. The shopkeeper warned the men in the shop that Mr Gardner was approaching. At the mention of his name I turned around. Papa looked straight at me, and I looked straight back at him, but then everything happened so quickly.

I ran into the shop, went out of the back door, and ran straight home. As I scurried into the house, I saw my mother. While I had my hands on my knees and gasped for breath, I told her that Papa was going to kill me for watching people gambling. She told me to go into the back garden and start chopping some wood. I'd chopped some wood earlier in the day, so I had a pile of wood around me when Papa got home, and it explained the sweat too. He asked my mother where I was, and Mama said that I had been chopping wood all day. I'm not sure that he believed her, but he let it go this time.

A law-abiding, by-the-book man, my father never gambled or bent or broke any law. After confirming my alibi with Mama, he went back to see Lennie. Papa warned Lennie about people gambling in his store. If it did happen, I was never to witness any of it.

But that hadn't been the first time I'd been watching, just the first time I got caught. I would watch the men in the bars, or sat on their patios, huddled over a small table playing dominoes, men would even gamble on a game of marbles. You could feel the tension as each domino was placed on the table, then the noise and excitement as they smashed the domino on the table, whether the person won or lost. Papa's warnings and my great escape weren't enough to put me off of gambling, but I never let him catch me again.

Chapter Two

I was fifteen and had just left school when the family moved to Springfield (St James). We moved into Sunnyside Cottage; it was the most beautiful place on Earth. Every morning I woke up with a smile on my face, opened the curtains and let the beautiful Jamaican sunshine through. If perfection exists in the world, it's at that little spot in Jamaica where every fruit seems to grow from the trees.

World War II had been raging for about two years when we had moved. The war didn't affect us directly too much, but it had become a backdrop in our daily lives. I was thirteen when it started. Like any Jamaican 13-year-old, I wasn't into politics and a war nowhere near the Caribbean was none of my concern. It was supposed to last two years, but no one was even mildly surprised when two years came and went and there was no end in sight. Every time you read the news or listened to the radio, there would be an update on the terrible war and a bleak report on how casualties were mounting. It seemed a million miles away, all this tragedy being reported to me while I looked for something to do in my Jamaican idyll.

Being new to Springfield, I didn't know many people and that was fine by me. I had my siblings of course, but they were busy with school or work; Gladstone was training to be a carpenter at the time. We all had our own lives and I got on with mine. I would eventually make some friends in Springfield, but even then I liked being on my own. I learnt to enjoy my own company in those early Springfield days when I didn't know what to do and didn't have anything to do. I would spend my days riding around on my bike or just going for walks.

My elder sister Minerva wanted to train to be a nurse, but she needed to pass her level 3 exam. I had failed the exam after three attempts, which meant I wasn't able to graduate. I failed because I did not want to learn about British history and to get your final grades you had to pass the history exam. The British history book we had was about two inches thick compared to the Jamaican history book which was more like a pamphlet. 'Why should I learn about long dead English kings and queens?' I thought.

So she asked me if I would help her with her studies, of course I said yes. In any subject other than history, I excelled. The only problem was that I thought that I would have to attend school with her. With the family being new to the area the staff at the school did not know me, they had no idea if I could even read or write, so they said no.

Mr Green was the headmaster at the school, I had already had a disagreement with him. I had been watching some boys playing marbles in the school yard, when suddenly I got this whack across the backside with a cane, 'what are you doing here,' he shouted at me. Not knowing who he was I turned around ready to hit him.

Realising he was a teacher I stammered that I was only watching them play. 'You are not supposed to be in here, now get out of my school yard.' That put paid to me helping Minerva at the school. We did work on her studies on evenings and weekends and thankfully she passed her exams and went on to be a nurse.

I was so happy for my sister, but it left me restless once again. I was still unemployed and restless, maybe I wasn't looking for purpose, but I did need to find something to kill time. My papa was right that uneducated men had an easier time finding work than women, but either way there just wasn't much work in Jamaica at the time. That was doubly true for Springfield. It was in the countryside, where there were no factories or large farms to employ staff. So I was left sitting around the house, going out riding my bike and helping my younger siblings with their education.

I also helped one of the local traders, Marsudol. He was good with money but had trouble with reading and writing. I would help him with writing his accounts and load his truck with bananas to be transported to the docks. Marsudol had four sons, one of them hated me. I know this because he told me plain, 'I hate your guts.'

He disliked that I was a policeman's son. He was jealous that I could read better than him and had a head for numbers, like their father; the boys had trouble reading and writing. He despised the fact that his father made him come and get me, so that I could help with any paperwork. Despite his open hatred for me, he was harmless, so I paid him no mind. I was used to jealousy and as long as you weren't beating me over the head, why would I care? It was his problem, not mine.

One day I was out walking when a truck with a few men on it went past. Having nothing to do I jumped on the back. You could do that kind of thing then; I didn't care where it was going. These men were lumber-jacks on their way to a job. I spent a bit of time with them, just watching how they felled a tree. I would do odd jobs for them, like make tea and getting them sandwiches.

Hitch hiking and jumping on trucks was common in Jamaica then. I'd do it every now and then if I felt like it. I never cared where they were going, it was just something to do. I never had so much free time in my life. So much spare time to do whatever I wanted, which was not a lot. I was always on the move, friends and neighbours would stop me to talk, but after a quick hello I was gone, I was not going anywhere in particular, just moving and moving quickly.

I would visit my grandmother, Gan-Gan as we called her, for days at a time to help her with her fruit trees and plant vegetables to help pass the time. She lived in Hopewell about twelve miles from Springfield. To get there I would walk along the road, getting a lift from a passing truck. It would take a long time, but it was worth it. I loved going to see Gan-Gan.

I also sang in a male voice choir, the Cambridge Male Voice, along with other members of the family, my father and nearly all my brothers were in the choir at some point. The choir would perform at various local events and sing at different churches. I enjoyed singing with the choir at the Moravian church in Springfield, it was at the top of a hill, and it had an organ which made the most wonderful sound. To this day I love the sound of an organ being played.

But soon after we moved to Springfield I stopped going to church. The church we went to in Cambridge was Wesleyan Methodist, which I liked, but the church in Springfield was Baptist. My parents were very religious. They grew up going to a Wesleyan church and we would go to church every week in Cambridge. They still went to church when we lived in Springfield but didn't insist that we go too. I went a few times to this new Baptist Church, but I didn't like the service and stopped attending soon after.

There was some gentle encouragement from my parents, every now and then they would make a comment about me not going, but they never tried to force me to go. I am not the most religious man, I have my beliefs, but there are two things that I never discuss and they are religion and politics, the two main things in this world that lead to trouble.

My father suggested that I consider joining the police force, but I was not interested. Then my parents encouraged me to try and get an apprenticeship in some kind of trade, but I wasn't interested in anything. My papa even went to the local sugar estate to ask if they needed an apprentice to work on the sugar processing machines, but at the time they did not need anyone.

I did think about leaving the island to go and work on a farm or factory in America, like a lot of Jamaicans were doing at the time. I tried to enrol, but I was told that I was too young and too small.

I went along to the local power station in Montego Bay. I was interested in the mechanics and how electricity was created and wanted to see if there were any vacancies, but again I was told that I was too young and too small. I know that I am not the tallest man on the island, but I could never understand what my height had anything to do with these jobs. I am five-foot-eight-and-a-half inches tall (178cm in today's world), I was fit, strong and used to work.

So, I spent about two years milling about and looking for purpose or even just something to do. It was a peaceful time in my life, I didn't even get into any fights, not having to protect my brothers and sisters, my life was trouble free.

Then at the age of seventeen, purpose came to me in the form of an advertisement for the Royal Air Force I saw in *The Gleaner* (the Jamaican daily paper). The advert was recruiting personnel to help in the war effort. We had read about the war in *The Gleaner* and we were always hearing about it whenever we were around a radio. I had no second thoughts; I knew that I had to do my duty. My father had done his duty in WWI, now it was my turn.

On attending the recruitment office, I had to do a medical test and an aptitude test. Doubt never crossed my mind, I never thought I'd fail either test. If I had, I'd probably have gone to the United States to look for work. How different things could have been. The medical test was simple, just checking baseline fitness to make sure we could do the training. The aptitude test was easy too, just testing basic literacy and maths.

I'd heard that many men and boys had taken the test in Kingston with only a handful passing, but it did not take me too long. I finished quickly then sat outside the recruiting office, talking to other men hoping to enlist. An officer came out and called out names, but I was too busy chatting. My name was the third one to be called out, but I missed it. Someone had to tap me on the shoulder to say they were calling my name. I went back into the office, where I was informed that I had passed the test and had been accepted into the RAF.

I came home pleased as punch. My father said to me, 'well son you are in the forces now.' Papa was a stoic man, an old school Jamaican, but I knew then that he was proud of me, but his words triggered something else in me. Up until I heard Papa's words, I had not given it much thought that I was really going off to a war zone. Now that I had signed up, I asked my friends if they were also thinking about it. I told them about the test, and they all said that there was no point, they did not believe that they would pass it.

I then had to wait a couple of months until I turned eighteen and could be officially called up. I spent the time saying goodbyes, splitting the time between our house in Springfield where I'd help Mum and in Hopewell, where I'd help Gan-Gan around the house.

I still remember getting my uniform. It wasn't the biggest milestone of joining up or the most exciting thing about serving, but it made it all real. I went to the base, a load of men already there and lined up. The man at the front looked at me up and down; in an instant he sized me up. *He must be an expert*, I thought, *knowing my size like a skilled tailor*. I wondered how many thousands of times he had done this.

He handed me my things and I went into a corner and changed in a hurry. I put it on ready to look like a soldier, ready to go to war and defeat Hitler, to save the world from Nazi Germany. It didn't fit. Clearly practice isn't a replacement for good eyesight, I don't think the man gave anyone their correct size that day. Mine was too big for me, but others might have well been swimming in their clothes.

I just went around seeing if someone was in the opposite situation to me and wanted to swap. The amount of people who said, 'What? No, you can't change it,' drove me crazy. 'What do you mean you can't change it? It's the same thing.' Eventually I found a man a few inches taller than me who was stuffed into his uniform. He was standing perfectly still, like he was scared moving would rip the whole uniform apart, I didn't blame him. He gave me the same first response as the others, but quickly realised how ridiculous he looked and that was that. I had my uniform.

The first time I went home in my uniform, I was beaming. I'd been excited since I'd passed the test, but now I could barely contain myself. I don't think I stopped smiling from the time I got my uniform until we went away. I could feel the neighbours watching me as I walked down the street. When the time came to leave home and join my squad, I was walking down the road with my friends from Montego Bay who had also been called up. Many of them were in the same boat as me, jobless, purposeless, and looking for excitement.

We discussed how we could manage to stay together when we joined, knowing it probably wouldn't work out, but excitedly planning and chatting and laughing all the same. The anticipation of going is sometimes the best part, when every situation you dream of seems possible and you don't know enough to know better. I didn't really think we'd see combat or that I'd fly or receive every commendation a hero can receive in war, but it's fun to dream with your friends. As we marched away from our childhoods, my mother cried out, 'Lloyd, you look after Ford!'

'I will, Miss Lou. You can bet!' he replied, and off we went.

Chapter Three

I am often asked if I was scared about going to England to help in the war effort. I wasn't. Nervous and apprehensive? Yes! We all were. We knew what was happening elsewhere in the world, on the odd occasion that we went to the cinema the Pathé newsreels before the film would inform us about the war. We also knew that if the Germans won the war, that people of African descent would be like the Jewish people and be next on the list for extermination and that millions would be enslaved. We did not want that to happen to our people ever again. I don't think that any of us were scared, otherwise we would not have signed up. We were young, strong, and ready to take on the world.

We did six weeks of basic training at Palisadoes. The basic training was composed almost entirely of square bashing, which was really just learning how to march.

When we had finally learnt how to march, we went to the docks in Kingston, where we set off to the UK. During our training we stayed in barracks around the airport, this was the first time that I had ever been away from my family. Surprisingly, I wasn't homesick. I was on an adventure, and I was enjoying it. I think then, it didn't seem like a goodbye, I was young and didn't even consider the possibility that I might not come back.

The first stop en route to the UK was Cuba. What should have been a short journey across the Caribbean Sea to Guantanamo Bay ended up taking four days. Halfway across the sea, the SS *Cuba* broke down and it took almost two days for the ship to travel the last miles before limping into port.

When we eventually reached Cuba, the ship stayed for about two days at the island before leaving for the United States. From Cuba we sailed to Newport News in Virginia, where we disembarked. We walked on to what we thought was the dockside, but in fact it was a large barge, which we only realised when it started to move. Everyone who was on the ship, including the captain and his crew, was taken to a large medical warehouse, where we were told to strip, and we were then sprayed with some type of disinfectant.

From there we travelled up to Camp Patrick Henry. I enjoyed my stay in the camp, especially the food and it was one of the only times in my life that I never finished a meal. The size of the pork chops! I didn't realise that pigs could get that big. We would be given half a chicken along with a plate full of vegetables. We stayed in Camp Patrick Henry for about a week, we did not have to do any training there, so all we did was get up in the morning, have breakfast, have a walk about the camp and go to the cinema, where we watched some Westerns and gangster movies, or we would do a bit of gambling.

We had to be careful where we went in the camp. One night I, along with a couple of other West Indian servicemen, was stopped from entering a dancehall one night. We started to argue with the guard but he made a movement towards his gun and so we left immediately. There did not appear to be any segregation between the West Indian servicemen and American servicemen, but there was between the white American servicemen and African American servicemen, and there was always the chance of trouble. We did manage to find a bar, which was full of black servicemen, there was a band playing some amazing jazz music, but still feeling unsure about things we decided not to go into the bar. We just sat outside and listened to the music.

So at the end of that week at Camp Patrick Henry we boarded a train to New York City. One of the things that I noticed after arriving or leaving the camps in the USA was that there was always a military band playing, there was one to welcome us, and one to see us off. We all felt full of pride watching and listening to the bands. There always seemed to be a crowd of people on the platform, waving the train off, they did not know us, we did not know them, but we would always smile and wave back.

I hoped that once we arrived in New York we would be able to have a couple of days to see the sights, but we went straight from the train onto the ship.

The troopship SS *Esperance Bay* set off from New York with me and the other raw recruits on board, full of excitement and apprehension, to the UK. As I got to know more men on the boat, I realised that it was not all young men, there were quite a few older more experienced men among us, including bankers, lawyers, policemen and teachers. One young recruit, someone who I became friendly with on the ship, a guy named Butler, met his old high school principal on the ship, and even though they were now of the same rank he could not bring himself to call him by his first name. He always addressed him as 'sir' or 'Mr Smith', whatever his name was. Every now and again the principal for a joke would shout out 'Butler', and Butler would stand up and say, 'yes sir' before realising he was being made fun of.

It took about twelve days to travel to the UK and, with it being a troop ship, there was not much to do. The only thing we could do when not gambling for cigarettes was talk and all we had to talk about was the war. We spoke about having to fight the Germans, how many we could kill, if any of us would become fighter pilots, I hoped I would.

The ship went north towards Greenland and this was the first time we West Indian servicemen started to feel 'real cold', the first time many of us had ever really felt it. Thermals, great coats, and woolly hats became the order of the day. Everything was frozen, you couldn't touch the safety rails without gloves on, we had to put on every item of clothing we could find. I count myself lucky, unlike some of my fellow colleagues on the ship, I did not get seasick and so I was able to spend time on the deck or in the galley. Always looking for any extra food which might be available.

The ship travelled in a convoy, so along with other troop ships there were also supply ships, carrying food and arms to the UK and there was always an escort of destroyers to protect us from attack from submarines. Those of us who were not seasick would sit and talk about the journey, none of us really knew what to expect once we arrived in the UK.

Thankfully, our convoy sailed without any enemy attacks. There was one incident on the ship I remember. I had been informed that a couple of the escort ships were going to have a live firing exercise of their big guns. We recruits had never heard the sound of big guns before so did not know what to expect. Unfortunately or maybe on purpose, nobody happened to mention it to the men below deck so when the guns were fired there was the loudest noise you could ever imagine.

They only fired about three rounds, but panic spread among those below deck, even among the men on deck who had not been told about the exercise. Everyone rushed up on deck thinking we were under attack, this was the first 'action' many of them had seen and they were losing their minds, people shouting, 'is it a submarine attack?' Some were already in their life jackets, many men on their knees praying.

The crew on the ship found it amusing, as did I and the other recruits aware of the gun firing exercise, but most of the West Indian servicemen were not happy when they found out that it was just an exercise they had not been warned about.

Also, I don't know if this was true, but I heard a story regarding another West Indian troop ship which caused a bit of a panic among the men on that ship. The ship was apparently in a convoy and during the night somehow became detached from the main convoy. A rumour went around that ship that they were a decoy ship being used to lure away the German U-boats, I can only imagine the panic and terror on that ship.

Chapter Four

The ship sailed into Liverpool docks on the 3rd of June 1944, three days before D-Day, there to meet us was the Secretary of State for the Colonies, Oliver Stanley and an RAF band. Even though it was June and the beginning of the British summer we still found it very cold. Once we had disembarked, we boarded a train to RAF Hunmanby Moor training camp, close to the North Yorkshire fishing town of Filey. The training camp was originally built for use as a holiday camp by Billy Butlin but was used as an RAF training base from 1939 to 1945.

The first thing I noticed about England was the cold. I knew England wasn't Jamaica, I wasn't expecting the warmth and the sunshine I was used to. But it was early June and I guess I had hopes for warmth and sun, even some mild weather would have been passable. Nothing in my eighteen years of living in Jamaica prepared me for the grey that covered the whole sky. No warnings could have prepared me for the biting cold. I realised then that I'd grown up in paradise. That isn't to say that I thought England was hell, hell is hot. I wasn't used to miserable weather, but I knew I'd adjust. I was in England now and would be until the end of the war, I had no damn idea when that would be, so what was the point of complaining?

Apart from the drab skies, what struck me the most was the chimneys on the houses. In Jamaica the only chimneys we saw were on the factories and the big plantation houses. At first this made us all think that there were hundreds of factories in the country and that there must be plenty of work in Britain. Being a country boy I was not used to seeing the large number of houses that were all grouped together in the inner cities, we don't have back-to-back or terraced houses in Jamaica, then the train ride through the countryside, seeing the fields, the Pennines, and the North Yorkshire Moors, I thought the countryside was beautiful, the woods and forests made it feel a little bit like home.

As we got off the train in Filey we were divided into groups of 50, and depending on the group you were in, that became your flight number. I ended up in Flight Five. This division into groups for training unsettled quite a few people because as we moved around the train, you could lose contact with your mates and end up being in a separate flight division from your friends. Others tried to move around and arrange it so they'd be in the same flight as their friends, but I didn't really mind where I ended up.

It could be said that my life story is not so much a life story, but a pattern. I manage to find myself in some trouble and just as easily and immediately, I seem to get out of it. It didn't take long for this pattern to emerge in the UK, I got into trouble my first night in England.

I was used to all the fine food and large portions during our week in the USA. When I was given only one small lamb chop with my first meal, I reached over the food counter and speared another two lamb chops with my fork. As I sat down, I was approached by an officer and two SPs (military police) who accused me of stealing another man's rations. I said something about it not being like Camp Patrick Henry in America and was told sternly, 'you are not in America now.'

As I was being spoken to, other recruits started shouting for the officer to leave me alone, eventually things calmed down and I realised that the large rations of steaks, pork chops and vegetables were a thing of the past. It took me a long time to get used to the small portions and the bland food in the UK, and I'm the kind of person who will eat anything and everything.

Basic training started straight away. I was good at marching; I think because I actually enjoyed it. Most of the soldiers found it monotonous, understandably, but I took pride in it, there are certain things in life that are really lovely. It's in the automation of the thing, how it becomes a natural and easy practice as you develop as a soldier. Some people found it monotonous, but I found a beautiful solitude in marching.

Passion is always recognised and I was placed in a group that was chosen, if required, to take part in ceremonial duties. I'm not sure if that was just a way to get us to do extra marching, but it was fine by me. However, after a couple of weeks, the trainers informed me that I was about two inches too small, all the other men were about six foot tall, (as I said earlier, I was five foot eight and a half inches tall) and unfortunately, I had to leave the team. In the end the team never took part in any official duties, due to members being posted to their various bases.

Among us there was another group of recruits who turned out to be exceptional marksmen. They formed a team, and their commander entered them into a competition at Bisley, the home of the National Rifle Association in Surrey. After a few weeks of practice, they were ready to take part, but at the last minute they were pulled from the competition. Reasons for the withdrawal were not given at the time, but it was believed that the authorities were worried that a team of West Indian marksmen could beat the best of the other British armed forces. I never found out who did win that competition and due to men being assigned to their regiments, the team of West Indians was disbanded.

One beautiful August sunny day still sticks out in my mind. It must have been the weekend because we were not doing square bashing or other duties. About eight weeks after arriving in the UK I, along with four other West Indians, fancied a swim in the sea. RAF Hunmanby is just about three miles from the beaches of Filey, so we had to go by bus to get there. Most of the beaches had been cordoned off with anti-invasion equipment, but we managed to find a small section of beach we could use.

We weren't sure if we were allowed to be there, but anyway we got our trunks on and ran into the sea thinking that as it was a nice sunny day the water would be warm, but the North Sea soon proved us wrong. As soon as we hit the water, we all screamed in shock and ran out of the water faster than we had run in, never to go back in again, and to this day I have never even paddled in the seas on the English coast.

When we first arrived in Filey, the Officers, Non-commissioned Officers (NCOs) and the local population were surprised by how different the West Indians looked, the different shades of skin colour and the different nationalities, with African West Indians, Asian West Indians and the Chinese West Indians. Often unfamiliarity and discomfort can turn into fear and hatred. I think some of my fellow troops anticipated being met with racism. Instead, we were met with open arms. The people of Filey and Hunmanby were very welcoming and really made us feel at home.

When we went on marches through the village of Hunmanby, the local people would come out to watch us marching. One day as we were marching down the main street one of our lads who was about 6 feet 6 inches tall bent down and picked up a small child, the little girl started laughing and called out to her mother, 'look Mam I have my own black man,' we all laughed, but the look of terror on the mother's face was one to behold.

There were four pubs near the base: The White Swan, The Cottage, The Horseshoe Inn and the Piebald Inn. I was not a big drinker, but many of my fellow soldiers were, so visits were fairly frequent. We didn't discriminate and patronised all of the pubs from time to time.

As it goes when you mix young men and alcohol, trouble would sometimes occur. It was not only the British or American service men we would clash with. Some of the lads decided to go to the White Swan. I don't remember having any problems in this pub, but whether you did or didn't have a problem on a particular night was more about who decided to show up at the pub, rather than which pub you were in. Some

French sailors at the pub decided to take exception to seeing West Indian servicemen enjoying themselves and started on them.

I was far from the action, drinking at The Horseshoe Inn that night. I only heard the story when I got back to base and saw some of my pals had been beaten black and blue. These West Indian men were small in stature and had come off worse in this encounter. Word about the incident spread quickly around the camp. Some of the bigger lads, and there were some big lads, decided that the French sailors were not going to get away with it. They went to the pub and sorted them out. We realised then that the life of a West Indian servicemen was not going to be easy.

Whilst training at Filey, some of the West Indians found it hard to take orders and were quite insubordinate. As in the days of slavery, we saw NCOs and the like as overseers and taskmasters, and I include myself in that. Since I was a boy, I've always been one to question authority. We found young officers to be very cheeky. By cheeky I mean they did not seem to show us West Indian servicemen any respect at all. Maybe this was the way they treated all recruits, but this was all new to us.

On one occasion, my friend Lawson and I were stopped by a young officer. We were not doing anything wrong; we were just chatting to each other. We may not have saluted him in the correct manner, who knows? Some people are too full of their own importance.

We were always being told to take our hands out of our pockets or to put our caps on correctly whilst walking around the camp. Anyway this time we answered back, some not very polite things were said between us, the officer called out to a couple of SPs to come and arrest us. We ran off into the nearest building, which turned out to be the cookhouse. Once in there we split up, but we both put on a cook's white coat, which we found hanging by the door.

When the officer and the SPs ran into the cook house, they asked us which way the two men went. 'Through that back door,' Lawson pointed. The Officer and the SPs ran out looking for the two men. We then took off the coats and walked off in the opposite way. This time we got away with it, but from then on, we were more careful with what we said to the officers.

Chapter Five

After doing the six weeks initial training at Palisadoes, Jamaica. I thought that I would still only be marching once we arrived at the camp in Hunmanby, how wrong I was. We marched, of course, that was most of what we did, but we also had to learn how to use small arms, rifles and Sten guns as well. The only weapon that I had ever used before was a catapult, so learning to use weapons that could actually kill people was an experience. There was also grenade training, where we had to stand in a hole/trench type of thing and throw the grenade at a target.

One day, whilst we were training to use a Sten gun, the airman holding it suddenly turned around saying that his gun was jammed. We all ducked down, some of the airmen throwing themselves on the floor. The instructor shouted at him to stop pointing the gun at the men behind him. He had no sooner turned back towards the target when the gun burst into live. He would have wiped out half of the men who were waiting for their turn if the gun had gone off a second earlier.

That was not the only time I could have died; I came closer to dying from friendly fire than I ever did at the hands of the Nazis. I was standing in line for grenade training. The man in front of me was so nervous he was shaking. I heard him pull the pin, but instead of throwing the grenade away he dropped it. Time slowed down as I watched it fall from his hand.

In emergencies like this, fight, flight, or freeze are the main responses.

The nervous man froze. He dropped the grenade and remained frozen, even now I can't say with certainty that he has moved from that spot. There are others who will always take a crisis by the scruff of the neck. I have no doubt there exist men in real life who, without thinking, maybe even against their better judgement would dive straight on that grenade, saving everyone around them. I am thankful that I am not one of those people, before the thing hit the floor I was gone; I had never moved that fast in my life. Thankfully the trainer was just as quick as me, but he moved towards the man. He picked up the grenade and threw it away. He must have seen that happen quite a few times before for that to be his first response. There existed no instinct in my body that told me I should go towards the grenade.

Despite these brushes with death, I enjoyed weapons training, particularly Sten gun training. A Sten gun is a British submachine gun, I found it easier to use than the big heavy rifle we had to train with. It was pretty much just pull the trigger and destroy. We all hoped that we would never have to use the weapons in a live situation but understood the reality of our situation. We needed to be ready for combat, but we were kept in the dark mostly and didn't know how it was going. We weren't on the frontlines and had no way of judging for ourselves.

When I'm asked how it felt to hold a rifle, I avoid the question. I couldn't feel the rifle, as my hands were so numb, some days holding it was the hardest part of training. The only consolation for the cold was after rifle training, we would march to the hangar where we'd be fed hot soup. It wasn't the best soup I'd had, but it was hot and that's all I needed.

Another part of square bashing was that we were taught how to make up our bunk beds, the sheets on the bunk bed had to be tucked in very tight. To check that the sheets were tight enough whenever there was an inspection, the Officer doing the inspection would bounce a coin on the bed to see how high it would bounce. If he was not happy with the height of the bounce, he would make you redo the bed. We also had to make sure that our uniform was kept in top class condition, that our lockers were spotless, and that all our uniform and equipment was in order. That is the reason why one of the first things I did was to buy an iron; to me looking smart was essential.

Training was a natural transition, as most of it was square bashing. When we weren't marching, we were assigned to different jobs and assessed. The assessment informed the instructors what type of job we were suitable for. I must have shown good mechanical aptitude because I was assigned to do a mechanical course. Some became chefs, others did electrical or radar courses.

After twelve weeks of square bashing and training to become a motor mechanic, some of my fellow West Indian trainees were being posted to their respective regiments. That took me by surprise because I was not assigned to a regiment. It turned out that those men had been assigned general duty postings (labouring, cleaning etc). Those of us who were doing mechanical and other technical courses were held back a few more weeks.

I was eventually posted to RAF Weeton to continue my mechanical training. This consisted of stripping and rebuilding engines, cleaning carburettors and spark plugs, this type of work was all new to most of us, but we did have a bit of inside help. One of my fellow recruits, a man called Forbes, had been a teacher from Kingston technical college who taught car maintenance and he knew more than our RAF instructor, but he never let on and would always help us if we had any problems.

Forbes was a bit of a joker, one day he came to me and said, 'hold these wires and wind that handle,' pointing to a handle next to him. Most of the men were older than me and already had technical experience, I didn't know any better. So, like a fool I wound the handle and got the shock of my life, I screamed and must have jumped about six feet in the air. The man had made a little transformer, so that when you turned the handle it gave you an electric shock. The other men in the room all fell about laughing. I was a bit thrown, but it was a joke, and I took it like one.

For some reason Forbes had taken a dislike to his instructor and was going to attach the wires to the door handle, so that when he walked into the room it would give him a shock. He had used me as his guinea pig to make sure that it worked. Thankfully this was fairly early on in my training, after that I was always careful if anyone asked me to do anything different to the job that I should be doing.

Weeton is in Lancashire and is near to the seaside town of Blackpool, where we would go for nights-out. We would also spend time in the towns of Preston, Bolton and Burnley all within a bus ride of the base. In the pubs and dancehalls, there was always the potential for trouble, not just with the American soldiers, but also with English soldiers and sailors who had come home on leave to find their wives or girlfriends out dancing with West Indians.

I have seven sisters, who all had friends who would come to the house. It was with these friends, especially the older girls that I became the flirt I was in my youth. So when I arrived in the UK, I had a good idea of how to behave and how to talk to the young ladies. I knew which girl to talk to and which girl not to talk to. I was not one for big chat up lines, no 'do you come here often?' or 'heaven must be missing an angel' rubbish, just talking to them was enough for a young lady to become interested in me.

So, whenever I was in the north of England, I always had a wonderful time. Meeting all the young girls and ladies. The people were so nice to us West Indians. So when we were on leave, we would book into the local YMCA in whichever town we were going to spend the night, but some-times we were invited to people's homes, that is if there was any room. In Bolton, it was the home of Suzy Hume.

I was introduced to Suzy through her daughter Joyce. I had met Joyce at the local dancehall and at the end of the night I offered to walk her home. When we got to the house, she asked me in. Suzy welcomed me in and offered me a cup of tea, and we sat, and we talked. She asked me where I was staying, I told her that I was staying at the local YMCA. She told me that she had a spare bed and that I could stay there, while on leave. I can tell what you may be thinking, dear reader, but I assure you this was just simple kindness from the women, nothing more.

Some people didn't see it like that. Someone sent a message to Suzy's husband, who was away serving in the army. They told him that a man had moved into his home. He came home unexpectedly one night, all geared up for an argument and possible trouble, only to find out that everything was innocent and above board, and that nobody had moved in.

With most of the men away the women were simply glad to have some company. The thing was that none of these women would take any money. The men who stayed in the house would leave money in places where our hosts would eventually find it. Suzy liked to have a drink, so when we saw her out in the pub, we would always buy her a drink.

The other nice family I met was in Burnley, Mrs Coney and her daughter Patricia, and the grandmother, or Grandma as we had to call her. I spent most of my leave in Burnley in their house. Sidney Foot, a serviceman who I had met on one of my courses, had introduced me to this family. One night I was at the house and the grandmother said to me, 'Young Gardner, you're coming with me, we are going old time dancing.'

At first, I said no, but she insisted. So off we went to the dance hall. As we entered, her friends all started to joke, saying things like, 'I see that you have brought your young man with you this week'. I was still only nineteen and all these older women were teaching me dances like the Gay Gordon and the Military Two Step, not my usual dances, but it was all good fun.

One night in the house Grandma said that she would have liked to have a photo of me. I did not have one, nor could I access a camera, but she said, 'I have one for you, it is of me and my granddaughter for you to take away.' I still have the lovely photo that she gave me.

I was a good soldier, but when off-duty I did what all my fellow soldiers were doing. There wasn't much in the way of entertainment, so we went to the pub a lot and we smoked a lot. Everyone smoked then, sometimes you could hardly see your friend next to you at the pub for all the smoke in the air.

I realised it was all too much after one particular night on the town. I spent the night drinking and smoking with my friends and got myself in such a state that I did not know where I was or what I was doing. By some miracle I found my way to the house. To this day, I do not know how. I could barely walk. When I got in, I just sat down in a chair, saying over and over, 'one of them will have to go, one of them will have to go.'

I woke up with the worst hangover in my life. It was almost welcome, a reminder of how stupid I'd been the night before. I didn't give up drinking, but I never got in a state like that again. Smoking was another matter. I had a packet of cigarettes in my pocket. I gave them to a friend and never smoked again. It turned out that cigarettes were the one that had to go.

Though it was mostly the drink that had gotten me in that state, smoking had definitely taken its toll on me. My father was a great runner and though I was never as fast as him, I considered myself a good athlete, always ready to play any game going, but the smoking had made me sluggish and prone to coughing fits. I enjoyed drinking and saw the value in drinking in moderation, but what was the value of smoking in moderation?

Why was I smoking at all? I thought to myself. It was simply to feed an addiction, every time I moved, I wanted a cigarette. Those past few months I seemed to always have one in my mouth. So, I stopped wasting my money and decided to quit. It was one of the best decisions I ever made.

Burnley became the place I would travel to the most when I was on leave. I had met a few young ladies there. Sometimes when we met up with the girls, we would take a trip to Todmorden, a town a few miles from Burnley, and we would go onto the Pennines and have a picnic and couples would go off by themselves to find a secluded spot.

One particular time I was in Burnley one of the girls invited me to a feast the following week. I said that I may not be able to attend, because I was not sure if I would be able to get any more leave. The girl insisted that I should try to get there. 'The Burnley feast is the biggest event of the year,' she told me. She made me promise I'd do my best to be there.

Back at camp I went to see the warrant officer, I told him that I had been invited to the Burnley feast. He didn't care. I offered to do extra duties and in the end he let me go, but I had to be back in camp by a certain date and time.

On the train up to Burnley all I could think of was the meat roasting on spits and being barbecued. I hadn't fallen in love with English food, but I've never been one to turn my nose up at a feast. The rations we were fed were just about sufficient, but they left me wanting. What a shock when I got there and saw the swings and roundabouts. It was then that I realised that what I would call a funfair, was called a feast in this country. All there was to eat was candy floss and toffee apples, not the large chunks of beef, chicken, or pork I was expecting. Boy, was I disappointed at the time, but I still enjoyed the feast.

One thing I noticed about this part of the UK, is that all the policemen were huge men. Not the type of men to argue with, at the time I did not realise that there was a minimum height requirement for policemen, at the time they had to be at least six foot tall. Every policeman you met was a hulking man you didn't want any trouble with.

One night we had been to the local dancehall, The Aspinall, when one of the local men started to make a scene. He had had a bit too much to drink and was shouting and swearing, using a lot of very offensive and racist language. He started off saying something like, 'damned American stole my wife, now bloody n*****s going off with all the women.'

He wouldn't shut up. He just kept on with his tirade of insults. The police had been called to eject him, but that left a lot of time for him to continue his rant. There's only so much a man can stand, we'd had enough of his foul mouth. So, I hit him. Right as the policemen were walking up the stairs the man tumbled down, scattering the policemen like ninepins.

Nobody was hurt, even the man I punched was relatively unscathed as they arrested him. The police spoke to me, but luckily no action was taken against me. I seemed to be lucky in that respect. Things would happen around me but for whatever reason I got away with things.

Unfortunately trouble was a two-way thing and some West Indians would go out looking for trouble. One night a few friends and I were in a pub in Bolton, it was a relatively quiet night, and we were having a good time. Then one of my friends adopted a stern look on his face, as if someone had insulted him.

'That man look 'pon me,' he said, pointing at a white man at the bar. We turned to see a man keeping to himself, quietly nursing his pint and not looking at any of us. Yet my friend was adamant that the man was staring at him. We managed to calm my friend down, but while alcohol can soothe some, it lights a fire in others.

'That man keeps looking at me,' my friend repeated, after the next round of drinks. Fearing trouble, we decided to leave. We made it outside when my friend declared that he needed to go to the toilet and stormed back into the pub. He came out in a few minutes, holding his back and clearly in pain. He had confronted the innocent man and gotten what he deserved. Unfortunately for my friend, the man, who had not looked at him the whole night, turned out to be an army instructor in hand-to-hand combat and a black belt in judo. I like to think my friend learned a lesson from this incident. Though his bruises eventually healed, we never let him forget his foolishness. What else are friends for? I don't remember him starting a fight again.

Chapter Six

From Weeton, for my first official posting I was sent to Moreton-in-Marsh in Gloucestershire. I arrived at the start of winter 1945. After a couple of weeks doing general vehicle maintenance, I was called into the office and given my first callout job. My sergeant asked me if I could drive and I told him I couldn't. At home I had no reason to learn how to drive and no real opportunity either. No one in my family had a car, at the time only the extremely wealthy had cars. A few people had a truck, which they only used to transport goods to the market or the docks, the truck was never used for pleasure.

As I couldn't drive, the sergeant had to get me a WRAF (Women's Royal Air Force) driver to take me out to my first job. I had to repair a snow plough that had broken down near the runway. When I arrived at the snow plough everything was frozen. I got out of the car to check the snow plough, but I could not even open my toolbox because my hands were shaking so much. I was such a sorry sight that the WRAF driver took pity on me and told me to get back in the car. She had to help me get back in and put my toolbox away because I could hardly move.

She drove me back to the mess hut where I was told to sit by the fire to get warm, while a WRAF Officer got me a cup of tea. The WRAF officer summoned my sergeant and asked why he had sent me out on such a cold night.

'Would you go out on a night like this?' she asked him.

'No,' was his reply, 'that's why I sent him.' The snowplough was eventually repaired but not by me.

Although I never passed a driving test I still learnt to drive. I was a mechanic in the RAF, I had to learn. The RAF put me through a basic test that allowed me to drive around the base but not on the open road. One day I was asked by an officer if I could drive, this time I said yes. He took me to a car with a trailer on the back.

'Could you put this car and trailer by that building over there and reverse the trailer to the wall?' he said, pointing to an office block.

'Yes, sir,' I replied.

Driving forward with the trailer was not a problem, backwards was another matter. When I tried to reverse, no matter which way I turned the steering wheel, the trailer would not go the way I wanted it to go. After watching me struggle for a few minutes, the officer told me to get out of the car.

'This is how you do it,' he said, getting behind the steering wheel. Within seconds the car and trailer were neatly parked against the wall. 'Would you like to try again?' he asked me.

'No thank you, sir,' quickly sprang from my lips. I suppose that I should have taken proper driving lessons and tried to get a driving licence, but I never had a real need to learn, especially after my service was over.

After a few weeks doing normal duties, I was sent back to Weeton to do a fitter's course. On arrival I received a letter from my mother who told me that my old school friend Dennis Reed was stationed nearby. When I had gone to sign as a RAF volunteer, I had asked Dennis If he was going to join with me. He had said it wasn't for him, so I was surprised by my mother's letter. We managed to get in touch with each other and we met up in Blackpool where we had some photos taken of ourselves in uniform. We then sent copies back home to our proud parents in Jamaica.

I would write letters home to my family every week, keeping them informed of the training and work I was doing. Mama would write back every week and she also sent me food parcels now and again. I must have told her about how bad the food was over here, so she would send me a little taste of home, and sometimes there would be a bottle of rum wrapped up in a bamboo joint to keep it from breaking.

One day I was sipping on some of the rum when a white man in my billet asked me for a drink.

'No, man you can't have any,' I told him.

'If you don't let me have a drink, I will cut open your kit bag and just take it,' he said in a nasty manner. I was in no mood to argue with a man pointing a knife at me, so I gave him the bottle and went for a walk. I had not been out long when a couple of SPs found me and frog-marched me to the office.

'Is it you that has a bottle of rum?' I was asked by the officer in charge.

'Yes sir, I have,' I answered back.

'Come with me back to your billet,' he ordered. At this moment I did not understand what was happening, having drinks in your billet was not an offence, as far as I was aware.

When we arrived at my billet, the officer opened the door, the whole place stank. The man had drunk nearly half the bottle of rum, but the rum had not agreed with the man. He was laid out on the floor, vomit coming out of one end, I won't go into detail, but you can imagine what was coming out of the other end.

The officer confiscated what was left of my bottle of rum and told me that I could have it back when I next went on leave. We all had to help clean up the billet, but it took a couple of days to get rid of the smell. On the bright side the man never asked me for a drink again.

Life in England wasn't always marked with conflict and tension, rarely in fact. Invariably there was the odd skirmish, but on the whole the English people accepted us, they knew we were there to help in the war effort. When trouble erupted, it was usually with the American servicemen, they were not used to seeing black people having so much freedom and mixing with white women.

The fights themselves never got too serious; weapons were never used. We were all young men many miles from home, we had to stand up for ourselves, and nothing settled an argument like a fist in the mouth, bang and he's out, no carrying on.

I was alone in a pub one night just having a quiet beer, when a group of white American servicemen came into the bar. The landlord, seeing that I was on my own and knowing of the hatred that some Americans had for black people, feared for my safety and he took me into his living room. His family was sitting there. I stayed with them for a few hours until the landlord thought it was safe for me to leave.

Now I know that not all-American servicemen had a dislike for black people, but we had to be careful. Thinking back I cannot remember ever getting to know an American serviceman on a friendly basis, and we were supposed to be on the same side.

I did try to be friendly with everyone though, as a matter of survival, but also of prosperity. I learned early on that you should always get to know the warrant officer (they were really the people who ran the camps, issuing passes etc.) and the sports officer (if you were good at sports, you could get special privileges and extra rations) when moving to a new camp.

Warrant Officer Martin was the main person I got to know at Moreton-in-Marsh. He was a friendly person and always told us to come and see him if we needed anything. Warrant Officer Martin was always riding his bike. Because he was good to me, I always made sure that his bike was cleaned and oiled. I never told him I did this. If he knew that I was the one looking after his bike, he never let on.

Time off your normal duties and better rations were standard fare for the sporty soldiers. It paid to be athletic, so I tried out for any team I could, football, cricket, you name it. The problem was that I was never picked to play in any of the teams. Due to professional sport not being played during the war years, many had signed up to join in the war effort. So, there were a few professional players at most camps, maybe that's why I never got picked.

At one of the camps Jack London, the heavyweight boxer, was doing some coaching. I went along to help coach. Mr London took one look at my hands and told me I'd never make it as a boxer, my hands were too small. I knew that I had a good right hand, (it had been used quite a bit since I landed in the UK), but I wasn't going to argue with him. I did help him on the coaching side, taking the boxers on runs and helping with sparring.

The cook at the camp was a boxing fan, he'd make a special breakfast for the lads who trained. We would get up early and go for a long run, somewhere between four and five miles. One day after being on a training run, I returned to the mess hall by myself. The cook asked me where the other lads were, I told him that they were fed up with the training runs and had stopped.

'No more special breakfast for them,' he muttered. 'From now on it's going to be kippers.' And that was the end of full English breakfasts for them. I hated the runs too, but felt they were worth it for the breakfast, apparently, I was alone on that one.

On returning to Moreton-in-Marsh, after another fitter's course at RAF Weeton, the warrant officer informed me that I would be transferred to a camp in High Wycombe. I was in trouble with a young officer before I even stepped foot in the High Wycombe camp. We usually travelled by truck from camp to camp, and as I was jumping off the back of the truck my cap fell off. As I was bending down to pick it up this young officer was shouting at me to get back into uniform. He had not given me a chance to pick it up. I gave him a mouthful back. I was only there for two days when Moreton-in-Marsh asked for me back.

I was also sent, along with my friend Sidney Foot, to AEC Engineering in Southall, Middlesex to do a diesel course. It was only a five-day course, and the RAF gave us some money for a bed and breakfast, but Sidney knew someone who was stationed at the local RAF camp. He got in touch with his friend to find out if there was any room on the base so that we could stay there. It would save looking for accommodation.

We were told that there was room, so we got in touch with the warrant officer, and we were given permission to stay at the camp, which gave us a little extra cash in our pocket. However, when we arrived at the camp the SPs in the guard house would not let us in, they had not been told about our arrival but after a call to the warrant officer we were granted access.

On the first day of the course, the instructor said that the best way to learn about the diesel engines was to go out with the drivers on test runs and then to examine the engines on our return to the factory. There were about nine or ten trucks which would set out in a convoy and just drive around.

We had only been out for about an hour when the driver said that it was time for something to eat and the wagons pulled up at a farmhouse. The farmer came out with some sandwiches filled with bacon. I couldn't remember the last time I'd seen so much bacon. So much for rationing. If you knew the right people and the right places to go, I suppose you could get anything.

At Moreton I met a chap called Wisdom and we became close friends. Wisdom was an electrician who had his own small workshop. I would quite often go sit in the workshop and strip down and rebuild various electrical components. One day between shifts I was in my billet, which I shared with seven other West Indians and six Englishmen, when some trouble started.

I didn't know how it started. Whether it was an argument between the white and black servicemen or black against black or two white men fighting, was irrelevant once the SPs were called. It was a mess of fists and fury, there was no time to work out who was in the wrong, the priority was keeping yourself safe. Before I knew what was going on, the first SP charged into the billet and I hit him, knocking him over a bunk bed. The other men were fighting with the other SPs, while I was processing the chaos.

I decided that the best part of valour was to get out of the way, so I got on my bike and got the hell out of there. As I rode away, I bumped into

Wisdom. As I stopped to talk to him a message came over the Tannoy for officers and NCOs with small arms (small arms means revolvers, not men with short arms) to attend the fighting in the billet. I understood that it was unlikely that anyone would be shot, but it still made me nervous, why escalate things with guns?

Once the fighting had been stopped, without a bullet fired, my name came out as being the ringleader of the trouble. The SPs came looking for me. I was still with Wisdom when they found me. The accusations started, but my friend Wisdom told them that it could not have been me who started the fighting, as I had been with him all day. So, I was spared the agony of a court-martial and a possible jail sentence, thanks to my dear friend Wisdom.

I met a lot of interesting characters while serving. I joined as soon as I turned eighteen, I was a man ready for the RAF, but in many ways, I was a boy. While I was not actively looking for guidance, there were many who would try to offer it. Maurice was one such man. Maurice was West Indian and for some reason he did not like us young recruits mixing with the white servicemen.

Maurice was a strange man. He would take us to one side and say things like, 'look I am an older man,' before giving us unsolicited, often bad, advice. That he was an older man was perhaps the only factual thing he ever said to me; he was about 40 years of age. 'I know what I am talking about, I am more experienced than you, these men do not want to know you,' he would continue.

He was always talking. He loved to say that he was an experienced man, that he lived through the war, and that he had done this and he'd done that. I don't know how he did anything when every word that came out of his mouth was negative. He was always saying, especially to us younger airmen, 'don't do this' or 'you can't do that.'

I understand he was an experienced man, but unfortunately these experiences had led to his life being ruled by fear. Maurice was one of those people who did nothing, I have no idea what he did in the RAF. He always seemed to be by himself and appeared not to have many friends. I could not get on with him and I didn't try to, I just let him carry on and do his own thing.

One example, there was a group of Australians who were always asking us to play sports, usually football or cricket. We jumped at the offer, especially me, though I did not make the teams I have always loved playing sports, particularly cricket. Maurice would start to carry on at us. 'No no,' he would start off, 'do not go with those men. I'm telling you all these men want is to beat you all up. I am a more experienced man. I know what I am talking about.' We accepted the Australians' offer many times and rather than being an elaborate plan to beat us up, we just played cricket. Perhaps Maurice was wrong about this one.

Another time, a man came to have a word with us. He told us that he was a writer and involved with the entertainment at the camp. He was writing a sketch which would include some West Indians and he was looking for performers. Maurice put his oar in again, claiming that the sketch would only show us West Indians in a bad way. Without seeing the script he claimed that the sketch would be full of racial language and that we would be portrayed as monkeys.

It turned out that Maurice, despite everything he said about the sketch, had wanted to be in it himself. I did not get involved with that kind of thing and never went to see the show. At the time, I saw Maurice as an impediment to my youthful fun, that's all he was to me, an annoyance. Looking back, I have a deep pity for the man.

Despite Maurice's best attempts, I had no problem with the white servicemen. All my life I've had no real problems no matter where I am. I can go anywhere. Problems are something I can't afford, so I do my best to avoid them. In the RAF, as with everywhere I've been, I have tried to keep my head down and mind my own business. If something happens and I can help, I help, if I can't I just don't bother.

I often wonder what happened to the people I met in those camps. There was an Australian pilot I had become friendly with. Unfortunately, due to the passage of time, I cannot recall his name. He went out on a mission one night and never returned. This must have been one of the last missions flown, because the war ended soon after, and I never found out what happened to him.

Not many, if any of the West Indian servicemen I came to the UK with saw any fighting on the battlefield. There were some who had arrived earlier in the war who became pilots or navigators, like Cy Grant the singer and actor. However, most of us worked on the camps, aircraft bases and navy yards to make sure that the fighting men had the equipment to do their job.

Duties at the camps were basically eight-hour shifts with most weekends off, unless doing guard duties. When possible, along with other servicemen I would head to London for the weekend. Despite these regular trips, I never grew to like London, I found the place to be too big. We spent most of the time going to clubs and dancing or going to the cinema.

Sometimes to make a bit of extra money I would work in one of the hotels, along with some of the other West Indian servicemen. I was able to get work at the Grosvenor or Lyons Corner House Hotel, washing up the pots, pans, and plates. We could earn up to an extra £2 a night, to supplement our RAF pay, which if I remember correctly was only about 10 shillings a day, roughly £30 today.

I was never happy with the RAF pay in the beginning, it was a pittance, but I made it work for me until I found myself making more. Getting a job was one way of making it work, gambling was another way, especially the horses. Off-track betting was illegal then, so we had to find an off-street bookie, which wasn't difficult. It was just another thing I did in my youth that I shouldn't have been doing, but luckily, I managed to get away with things.

One of the jobs I was given when I worked at the Lyons Corner House Hotel was checking the fruit pies that were being delivered. I was told if there were any broken pies, I could eat them. When the boss came back, he noticed that I had not eaten any of the pies. When he asked me why I told him that none of them were broken. He laughed and told me I was the first one not to stuff myself with pie.

When on a night out in London, I always preferred the upmarket clubs if we could get in. At camp I made the acquaintance of flight sergeant Johnny Burke, who took me under his wing. He was a Jamaican liaison officer who had come to our camp because there had been quite a bit of trouble between some black and white servicemen (this time it was not me) on the base.

Johnny was one of the nicest Jamaicans I ever met, and one of the tallest too, he was about 6'7. He was a man after my own heart, he liked England because he loved horse racing. Here there was a race meeting he could bet on almost every day except Sunday.

Johnny would take me to clubs that were supposed to be only for officers and NCOs, he must have had contacts at these clubs, because he had no trouble getting me in. It was because of these clubs that I acquired my nickname. My fellow servicemen started to call me 'Baron' when they found out where I was going and who I was going with. I had a few nicknames actually.

Depending on who you spoke to, I was Alf, Gardie, Fordie or the Baron. This would occasionally cause some confusion when someone was looking for me. Some of my closest friends could have looked you dead in the eye and swear they did not know a Gardie. They'd have pointed you straight to me if you asked for Alf though.

There were a lot of clubs in those days, but without a doubt the best was the Caribbean Club. It was a very exclusive club, this was where the gentry of the day would frequent. The top jazz artists like Stephane Grappelli would play there and I would have the time of my life.

The club was near Buckingham Palace, and sometimes when I was in there with Johnny, you could hear people asking if the two girls were in that night, meaning Princess Elizabeth and Princess Margaret. Princess Elizabeth was never in when I was there, but I'm sure that Princess

Margaret was. I think she asked me to dance one night, or perhaps it was a lookalike with a really posh voice.

Of course, my time in the RAF wasn't all fun and games, as much as I tried to make it so. One of the duties I was given at Moreton-in-Marsh was looking after the beacons. This job was important, but for some reason nobody liked doing it. The war was now over so the beacons, which are the lights on the runway, could now be kept lit all night for returning aircraft. The person on the job had to stay awake all night, to make sure that the generator kept working.

There were only two of us on this assignment, the other man was a Welshman called Harry, an electrician and a drummer in the RAF band. He was not popular with other airmen, but no one ever told me why and I couldn't work it out for myself, I never had a problem with him. We had to spend the night in a caravan near the end of the runway, but it was large enough for us to have our own space.

I decided to make this assignment work for me. I went to the flight sergeant and made him an offer. I said, 'if I work seven nights, can I get seven days leave?'

'No,' was the answer I got back. I kept asking about leave; he told me you will get it when you are entitled to it. After three weeks of looking after the beacons, I went and asked for seven days leave again, and the flight sergeant said yes this time.

Two days after returning from leave, I was called into the office and told that I had more leave coming to me. My flight sergeant told the warrant officer that I had just come back from leave, but the warrant officer was not aware of that and gave me some more, so I was off again. My flight sergeant was not happy about this, saying, 'Gardner, you appear to be off base more than on it.'

I simply laughed because it was true and then I went and enjoyed myself on leave. In the afternoons I would go to the bookies. They weren't as common then. You had to know where to find them. At night I'd go dancing.

The first night working on the beacons I went to the cookhouse to get the rations for the both of us, I could not believe what they supplied for two men to last all night. I picked up the small tin with the food in it, there were two slices of bread and a bit of meat. So of course, I had no option but to complain. I went to my sergeant and plainly asked him, 'what is this?'

'That is your rations for the night,' came the reply. I kept calm. I said that it was not enough for the two of us. In the military, some see any action from a subordinate as a sign of disrespect. The effect is that anytime you raise an issue with a superior, they may choose to take offence and fly off the handle if they see fit. I think this is intentional, so that no one ever speaks up, but this wasn't right and I had to speak up, consequences be damned. My sergeant started to shout at me, saying that the war had only been over for a matter of months, food was still being rationed, and that was all we were allowed.

I assume he thought that was the end of it, but he underestimated the determination of a hungry man. I took the matter higher and went to the flight office and saw the Flight Lieutenant on duty that night. I showed him what we had been given to eat, he could not believe that was all they had given us to last the night. He took me in his car to the cookhouse, called for my sergeant and really told him off, saying that the men watching the beacons had to be alert all night and needed proper rations. Better rations, including tins of beef or ham, cheese, and milk, and more than just two slices of bread were provided every night from then on.

We did have one major incident; a plane overshot the runway one night and crashed into a farmer's field, killing a few chickens. The pilot was unharmed, but the dead chickens were spread over the end of the runway and the farmer's field. We asked the farmer what he was going to do with the chickens, he said that he would just burn them. We asked if we could take the ones that were not too badly damaged, he said that we could, which pleased the cook and the men who were able to have some fresh meat.

The farmer would sometimes sell us eggs. He never sold them to an Englishman, only to the West Indians because he could be sure we weren't food inspectors. Because of rationing he always had to be careful with who he was dealing with. To return the favour we would sometimes sell him any excess fuel we had left over after filling the generator for the lights.

Chapter Seven

My brother, Gladstone was in one of the last batches of recruits from the West Indies. I believe that he arrived either late 1944 or early 1945. After his initial training, he was stationed at base Melksham in Wiltshire, which was not too far from where I was stationed. Every now and again, duties allowing, we would meet on a weekend and head into London.

On one occasion we had arranged to meet up, we both set off from our respective bases and independently had the idea to hitchhike. By luck we arrived at the same crossroad within minutes of each other. I would hitchhike a lot, quite often it would be someone in a Rolls Royce or a Bentley who would pick me up. I suppose that in that part of the country it was only the well-off who could afford a car, and I would then be asked plenty of questions about life in the West Indies and what it was like for me being in the UK.

The most elegant Rolls Royce stopped to give me a lift once. I got in and exchanged pleasantries with the driver. This was the nicest car I'd ever seen, let alone been in, they didn't drive anything like this in Jamaica. I stayed cool though and got to chatting with him about the car and its engine, he was happy to talk about how powerful his car was, I couldn't blame him. Then he told me he was the first fighter pilot shot down in the Battle of Britain. He'd gunned two of them down, but one had got him. His injuries had left him disabled.

The top was down and it was a nice day. We were near Oxford on our way to London and I anticipated a nice drive as we crawled along the empty streets. This man had something else in mind. He asked me where I was going, I told him Westminster. That was near where he lived, so he said he'd drop me right to the address. The instant he stopped talking, he kicked it up a gear. Then another and another. I'd never gone so fast in my life. There were no curves in the road to London, just straight road to tear down. The car flew at certain points, you cannot convince me otherwise. It felt like we were flying the whole time.

I met some very nice people hitchhiking. I think people were a lot different back then. People were very helpful. If I needed something then it seemed like I just had to ask.

I never really liked London. I was stationed near there for a while and so naturally we would go for nights out there, but it was just something to do. I don't like big cities; I suppose that I will always be a country boy at heart. With so many servicemen now returning home thanks to the end of the war, the night clubs in London started to add restrictions, groups of men were not allowed into some dancehalls, and guys on their own had to be accompanied by a young lady. So I stopped going as much, and thanks to free train travel warrants I would make my way back to my old haunts of Blackpool, Burnley, and Bolton.

May 8 1945 may be a date familiar to you from your history textbooks. It was Victory in Europe Day, a.k.a V-E Day, and Gladstone and I managed to be in London together on the day. We joined the festivities taking place on the Mall, the road leading down to Buckingham Palace. We were both in our RAF uniforms that day and as we were walking down the Mall an RAF officer stopped us and asked us what we were doing, quick as a flash Gladstone turned to him and said, 'special duties, sir.'

'Carry on,' replied the officer, so we carried on down the Mall to Buckingham Palace to join in the celebrations. What a day that was. The crowds were singing and cheering, everyone hugging each other. The

largest cheer of the day was when the King, Queen and the two princesses, Elizabeth and Margaret, made their appearance on the balcony of
Buckingham Palace.

The outpouring of relief that day will be something I will always
remember. Whenever they show pictures of the V-E day celebrations
outside Buckingham Palace, I always try to spot Gladstone and me, but
so far, I have not been able to see us.

With the war now over, both Gladstone and I, in our respective squad-
rons, were employed in repairing and servicing motor vehicles. Though
the war was over, we were still needed. We were living on borrowed time,
and I intended to enjoy myself as much as I could while I was still here
and make as much money as possible.

One day I was the duty fitter on standby, when I was called to the
office. A car was having some problems and would be on base shortly, but
I would have to stay in the office until I was called. This was unusual but
I knew better than to question the situation.

The car turned up. It had a driver and four passengers, three females
and a man. The car was en route to Gloucester. The passengers got out
and were escorted to the mess hall. Once the passengers were out of sight,
I was called to look at the car. I started the car up and soon diagnosed the
problem. I stripped out the carburettor, gave it a good clean, put it back
on and started the car up, job done. I was told to go back to the office
while the passengers returned from the mess hall. The car drove off and
an officer came and told me that the passengers had thanked me for being
so quick and efficient.

Now I am not 100% sure, but because of the secrecy and security
surrounding the passengers, I have always believed it was King George
VI and his wife, along with the two princesses, Elizabeth and Margaret.
Another close call to meeting the royal family.

Chapter Eight

Then in late 1946 I was called into the warrant officers office and asked if I would like to do an engineering course in Leeds. It would be a six-month training course, where I would learn how to use a lathe, milling machines and radial drilling machines, the machines that were used in engineering factories at the time. I said yes, knowing that any extra training could be beneficial. They explained that even though I was still in the RAF I would be attending the course as a civilian, so I was able to wear normal clothes and not a uniform.

I accepted the offer, and was sent to a hostel in Knottingley, which is a small mining town to the east of Leeds. When I arrived, the hostel was full of Polish workers. As I walked into the hostel the men gave me a funny look and started talking to each other in their own language. Though my knowledge of Polish is non-existent, I think they were talking about me.

The man in charge of the hostel took me to one side and said that I was probably in the wrong place. He allowed me to stay the night, as it was too late to find anywhere else, but thought it would be best if I found other accommodation. Thankfully, I did only stay the night, and to be honest I felt a little bit uncomfortable, there would have been no one to talk to. I soon realised that the journey to the training course in the centre of Leeds would be a bit of a nightmare, it was a journey of about

21 miles, and we didn't realise at the time that it would be the start of the worst winter to hit the UK in decades.

On leaving the hostel I caught the bus to Leeds; it had been snowing and I was very cold. I had been given the name of the new hostel in Leeds that I had been assigned to, but I had no idea where the hostel was. I was always told that if you need to find somewhere or something in England, always ask a policeman. When I got off the bus at Leeds bus station, I began walking, looking for a policeman.

Eventually I found one, he was hard to miss. The man was a giant and went over to the large man to ask him for directions. He looked down at me and said, 'nay lad, you're not really prepared for this weather.' His Leeds accent was thick, but I'd gotten used to a variety of accents since enlisting. After living in England for over two years, I thought that I was getting used to the weather. I knew it'd be cold, so I had a big coat and hat on, but my shivering betrayed me. He was right.

'Come on, son. I'll take you to get a warm cup of tea and something to eat.'

'No, sir, I'm fine. I just need directions to my accommodation,' I replied through chattering teeth.

'Nay, lad. You need something inside you.' He took me into Leeds market to get warm and he bought me a cup of tea and a sandwich. I told him my story and that I had to find the hostel. He sat with me, and we spoke for a while. I told him that I needed to find a place called Greenbanks. I had the address on my order sheet. 'It's alright, son. We will get you there,' he said. We stayed there a bit, me finishing my food and getting comfortable while we chatted some more. Once I had warmed up, he arranged for a taxi to take me to the hostel.

With all the snow that had fallen over the last couple of days, the taxi was unable to take me to the front door of the hostel. I'm surprised he got me that close to the building. The hostel was in Horsforth, a suburb on the outskirts of Leeds. After tramping through the snow, I found my way to Greenbanks Hostel. Greenbanks was built in 1941 to house about 900 workers for the AVRO aircraft factory in Yeadon, they were building Lancaster bombers (these are the bombers used on the famous Dambusters Raid). It was now also being used for training purposes.

Once I was settled in my room, I went to the common room area where I met some fellow West Indians who were also doing various courses. On the weekends we'd spend our time at the Mecca and Mark Altman dance halls. There were six dance halls at the time in Leeds. We went to all of them, but on Saturday night, the Mecca was the place to be. With our accent and West Indian dance moves, we became quite popular with the local girls. It was much to the dismay of the local young men and unfortunately trouble would sometimes come our way.

Some people seemed to come just to cause trouble. Me? I never got into a fight at the Mecca. Not even an argument. I came to dance with the girls. Not even an argument. The girls would always come in groups, some in twos and threes, but most were in large groups. There would be a whole group, dozens of girls, standing around and not dancing, sometimes they wouldn't dance at all. I would go over to them and eventually convince one to dance. When the dance was done, another girl in the group would want to dance with you. Then the next one. Then they all wanted to dance with you.

No one in Leeds could tap-dance as well as me. The Mecca became my main haunt and I soon got to know the other regulars, the ones who came to dance too and were good at it. I'd have one girl who I'd always tap-dance with and another I'd always do the waltz with. Others I'd avoid like the plague because they had two left feet.

In the hostel there were workers of both sexes living there. Not long after I arrived at the hostel, a group of girls arrived from Scotland to work in one of the factories. They did not seem to like us West Indians and kept well away from us. I don't believe that they were racist, they were just not used to being around black people, but one of them was keen to know where we went on a weekend and followed us to the Mecca one night.

After reporting back to the other girls, they went back to Scotland, only to return a week later with new clothes, all ready to go dancing. A couple of them even ended up with West Indian boyfriends.

I got to know a lot of English people during my time in the UK, and when I was doing this course in Leeds I would go to a little shop near to the training centre, where I met a wonderful woman and her family. Mrs Noble was her name, she made me feel so welcome. The first day that I walked into her shop, she asked me if I would like a cup of tea, and she always made sure that I had everything I needed. We would sit and talk, she would tell me about her life in the UK and I would talk about my home and family back in Jamaica.

I had been to a few places in the north of England but never Leeds before now. According to some men at the places I was stationed, Leeds was a place to avoid. But during my time on the engineering course, I found that it was an entirely different place to what I was told. I found Leeds to be a very nice place filled with friendly people. As in Bolton and Burnley, the older women really looked after me, I think it was because of my baby face.

During my time doing my engineering course I became friendly with three young ladies who I had met at the Mecca dancehall, Norma, Florence and Margaret. Florence had met Norma and Margaret in the Mecca and the three of them became close friends and were always together. They were lovely dancers and we got to talking. I've always enjoyed my life to the fullest and met a lot of women in my time, but these three were special to me. Now when I say special, I mean special.

Florence was eighteen and one of the young ladies from Scotland. She was sharp as a tack, a beautiful young girl, with raven-black long hair and sharp, black eyes, who would have nothing to do with black men until she met me.

Margaret was a brunette. The shortest of the bunch and the most extroverted, she was the life of the party. I knew early on that her father did not like black men, he had told her that East is East and West is West and never the twain shall meet. In those days, what your parents thought always had a bearing on your own thoughts. She was a good dancer and though her father's beliefs weighed heavily on her, we were friends.

As for Norma, she was the quiet one of the three, but she always lit up a room. People took notice of her and you could tell that she was a strong young lady. She had the same shoulder length mousy-brown hair as Margaret and warm-brown eyes. A beautiful woman. She was five-feet-four-inches and had a slender figure. She was from a white working class family but didn't volunteer information about her father's preferences as readily as Margaret did to me. They all loved to dance, but Norma was the best dancer of the bunch, perhaps even a better dancer than me.

Dancing was the main thing at this time, young people did not go to the pub like they do nowadays. I suppose soldiers drinking and going to pubs is an eternal truth though, but if I had the choice, I'd go dancing over the pub any day. So, Friday and Saturday nights were the time to let loose. The managers of the dance halls were extremely strict on the type of dances we did; they did not like us jiving, but we would do anyway, if the right song were played. In this early post-war era jiving was deemed a little bit risqué, so it was more ballroom dancing, however, this brought the couples closer together, which defeated the object of the managers fears of couples getting too close.

I ended up getting close to all three of these girls, especially Florence, who became my girlfriend, but the other two were never far away. Florence and I had a lot of fun together, but it was also very casual and never exclusive. We knew from the start that our relationship was doomed, I'd be leaving soon, I guess that made everything seem more urgent. So, while this was an important relationship in my life, neither of us ever let it get too serious.

Still, they were all upset when the engineering course finished and I had to return to my new base at RAF Colerne in Wiltshire. I promised Florence that I would return as often as possible. However, when I returned to camp I was informed that all leave was being cancelled, with some West Indian servicemen going AWOL.

When I returned to RAF Colerne after completing my engineering course in Leeds, everything seemed to be winding down on the base. I could see the writing on the wall, my time in England was coming to an end. For the first two weeks I was not assigned any duties, I didn't even have a uniform, I was just riding around the base on a bike that I had acquired; it was like I was sixteen again. I'd found the bike lying around the base, it must have been left by an airman who had returned home. There always seemed to be bikes left lying around the base, you would make enquiries about it and if no one owned it, you would take it, fix it up and use it for yourself.

Towards the end of the second week of me doing nothing, I was riding past the warrant officers office, when he called me into his office, 'Now Mr Gardner, why are you not in uniform?' he asked me.

'Since I came back from Leeds, sir, I have not been issued with one,' I replied.

'You cannot keep riding around the base in civilian clothes, go to the stores and get yourself kitted out,' he said and passed me a kit deficiency card.

So off I went to the stores, on duty that day was a little Trinidadian man. Now there has always been a bit of rivalry between the men from the different islands so I thought that I would have a bit of fun with him. I went up to him and told him that I wanted a beret, a peek cap and the good shoes.

'No. Man, I can't give you all that,' he argued.

'Those are the things I want,' I insisted.

This conversation went back and forth for a while, with each response the Trinidadian became more tired of me and more exasperated. He started talking to me like I was an idiot, getting more confused as I refused to understand. Then I showed him the deficiency card, which had all the items I was asking for. He read the deficiency card, then looked at me. I could see he was fuming, but he retrieved the kit and dumped it in front of me, not saying one word the whole time. He didn't even acknowledge me when I thanked him and said my goodbyes.

Once I was settled in the camp, I wrote to the girls and told them that it was likely we'd never see each other again. When they wrote back, they were quite distraught. Florence asked if anything could be done so that I could get some leave. I went to see the warrant officer again, I told him that I had no intention of staying in the country and that I wanted to go back home to see my family, when my time to go back to Jamaica came around.

I was telling the truth, but he just said that he had heard the same excuse from other servicemen and the orders were, 'no leave for any West Indians.' I wrote to Florence again to say sorry. I would not be returning to Leeds.

She wrote back to say that she was going to get the train to come and see me, but that would have been impractical. She would not have been allowed to stay on base and we would never have been able to book a room in a hotel. I wanted to say yes and snatch at this little time that we could get together, even if it was just for a few minutes, even if it wasn't perfect. I missed her. But I couldn't ask her to come all that way for a few moments together, so that idea was shelved.

We didn't stop writing though. They all wrote to me. After about four weeks of writing to each other, the girls concocted a story to try and get me some leave. I was called into the warrant officer's office. He had received a telegram to say that Florence had been taken ill.

'Do you know anything about this, Gardner?'

'No, she didn't say anything, but it's been a few days since her last letter.'

'It says she's in a very bad state and is asking for you to come right away.'

'What's wrong with her? Can I go and see her?' I said. If I'd thought about it for a little bit, I'd have realised that Florence was fine and dandy, but being told like this by my superior, it didn't occur that Florence was hatching a scheme. I was scared and the warrant officer could see it. As we were talking another telegram arrived, supposedly from a doctor, saying how serious Florence's illness was.

The warrant officer looked down for a second. Then he apologised again, making sure to avoid eye contact, but he had his orders. There would be no leave for me. We carried on speaking for a while, I pleaded with him. I begged him, trying to convince him that I really did want to go back home to Jamaica. He finally relented and told me that he would see what he could do.

Those next few days I lived in a half-state, almost a state of denial. When I left the office, I considered that it was a ruse, but doubts plagued me. Why hadn't she told me? What if it was deadly serious? I eagerly awaited letters that never came, hoping for clarity.

A couple of days after I'd been called into the office, the third telegram arrived. Florence had taken a turn for the worse. I don't know if the warrant officer believed in any of it, if he was tired of the telegrams or if he did at least believe that I was a man of my word and did plan to go back to Jamaica, but he let me go on leave. I was on the first train back to Leeds to meet up with Florence and the girls.

I had a strange agitated excitement, by now I'd almost managed to convince myself that this was all just a scheme, a clever one, at that, since it had worked and allowed me to act as if I was genuinely worried and surprised because I was. However, the 'what ifs' plagued my mind until I finally saw Florence and held her in my arms.

Because I returned to camp when I was supposed to, I was able to get leave on a couple of more occasions. The last night of my final leave in Leeds was very emotional. Tears were shed as we confronted the fact that it would be the last time we would see each other. Back at base I packed my things ready to set sail home.

So my time came to be demobbed, I was keen to get back and see my family again, but it felt like I was leaving a piece of me behind. I'd miss the girls and I'd miss England. Not the weather, but the people. When you're young you don't think about the future, I never really thought about leaving everything behind right up until I had to. Some men remained in the UK and I understood the urge, but that thought never crossed my mind. Jamaica was my home.

Chapter Nine

I sailed back with Gladstone on the SS *Almanzora*. There wasn't much to do on the ship but gamble and tell stories. Gladstone and I talked a lot about our feelings about returning. We both felt excited to return. Still we'd miss England and the more we talked about it, the more we realised this wasn't goodbye. Our future in Jamaica was uncertain, but everything seemed so clear when we thought about a future in England. We could build a life there.

We arrived back in Kingston in December 1947, just in time for Christmas. It was a very different journey back home to Jamaica. We were not the young boys who had set out to war, we were now men. We were proud of our service and of doing honest work in England.

We would go back to Cambridge the next day, but we had to spend a night in Kingston. I made the most of it. I went to the Glass Bucket, a club in Kingston. I was barely eighteen when I went to war, so I'd never been there or to any club in Jamaica. There was less modesty than in England, the differences didn't surprise me though, it was the similarities that shocked me. The shy girls in groups, the men there just to cause trouble, the same sticky floors near the bar. I paid them no mind and danced the night away, just as I did in England.

The first night was saved for reconnection, we regaled each other with stories, talking and laughing all night. Gladstone and I told everyone about England and the war and everyone told us what had been going on in Jamaica in our absence. That first night back at home was one of the happiest nights of my life. I had my young brother Sam on one knee and my sister Mel on the other and we were all in tears. Hugs and kisses from my other sisters and my mama and papa; it was the only time I ever saw him cry.

Gladstone and I set about looking for work the next day, me as a motor mechanic and Gladstone as a cabinet maker. One of the main reasons we and so many other Jamaicans had left was because there was no work. Unfortunately that hadn't changed. There were not many vacancies anywhere in either profession. I had an uncle who was working in a factory at the time, I asked him to see if he could find me anything as a motor mechanic or working in the factories. He did his best, asking around, his friends, his boss, people on the street that looked like they had connections. Nothing. He said he might be able to get me something in a few months time. I didn't mind waiting, but I couldn't belive it when he told me the wage. To this day I still believe he must have been joking. I was making my own enquiries at the time, asking friends and family if they knew of any jobs, going down to local factories and companies, asking if I could even just work in the mailroom. There was almost nothing on offer. The little that there was were very poorly paid jobs that were oversubscribed due to the thousands of ex-servicemen returning to the island, all looking for the same type of jobs.

I'd hoped to settle in Jamaica for a while before I went back to England, to stay with my family, help Gan-Gan and watch my younger brothers and sisters grow up, but it wasn't an option. Not having a job, hitchhiking and biking was fine for a 15-year-old, but it was no way for a man to exist.

Just a couple of days after I arrived home, I told my parents that I was thinking about heading back to the UK. They were not surprised, but I still think my father had hopes for me following him into the police force. I now had the discipline to be a policeman thanks to the RAF training, but the corruption my dad had told me about the police force put me right off it.

I had not been back long before letters started to arrive from the girls. I wrote back to them and we just said the usual things people wrote to each other, how are you, when are you coming back, I miss you. All I could tell them was that I was fine and that I did not know if I would ever return to the UK.

I didn't want to get their hopes up and though at times I was resolute, at others I couldn't imagine leaving. Going back to England felt so permanent, when would I be back? When would I see everyone again? I would think of Gan-Gan and my parents, I'd probably never see them again. I was scared to leave, but it seemed I couldn't stay.

Now back home, unemployed and having nothing to occupy myself, I was working in the garden one day when we received a message from my sister Lynn. In March 1948, Lynn was at school in Kingston, sharing a house with someone who worked in an office on the docks. Lynn's housemate had heard about a ship that was going to return to the UK. Lynn phoned our local post office in Springfield, (our homes did not have phones in them days), to let Gladstone and I know about the ship.

Then an article appeared in *The Gleaner* that the UK was short of workers and was asking for West Indians, especially ex-servicemen, to return to the Mother Country to help to rebuild the country. It turned out that the advert had been placed by the captain of the ship in an effort to make money. I only found out about this deceit when I took part in a TV documentary by David Olusoga in 2019, *The Unwanted: The Secret Windrush Files*. At the time we thought that it had been placed by the British government. I have been asked how that made me feel, but to be honest I never gave it much thought, it all worked out for my fellow travellers and me.

The price was £28, about £800 in today's money. Gladstone had the money to buy a ticket. He didn't hang around and was soon on his way to Kingston to book his passage. Unfortunately I did not have the money, so

I went to ask my mother if anything could be done, she told me to go and see my father. My father told me to meet him at the bank in Montego Bay, where he gave me £50. I had my British/Jamaican passport, I packed my bags and a few possessions and I was ready to travel.

That last night before leaving Jamaica was a sad night, nobody knew when we would all meet again, and there were a lot of tears. My mama cried like I'd never seen her cry when I told her I was leaving. She'd accepted that I'd have to go eventually, but didn't want it to be so soon. I'd barely returned and already I was leaving again. She eventually accepted it though, after making some money in the UK she thought I would be back within a few years, that was the plan.

Like most parents, you know that your children will leave home at some time and they knew that there would be more opportunities for us in the UK, so they did not try to stop us from leaving. I felt the UK calling to me, but what really pushed us to leave was the lack of opportunities. I had to leave and if it hadn't been England, it would have probably been the United States.

The ship, which was called the *Windrush*, had already been to some of the other islands in the West Indies to pick up passengers before arriving in Jamaica and I was surprised to meet so many ex-servicemen returning to the UK. There were Trinidadians, Barbadians, Guyanese and others, but the majority of those returning to the UK came from Jamaica.

When I arrived at the docks there were dozens of men milling around the place, many hoping to buy a ticket. A rumour went around the men, saying that the ship was full. I could feel the panic start to rise within the crowd and everyone became tense, but someone said that it was a troop ship and it couldn't possibly be full. We all started to relax a bit then.

The ship had been moored in the harbour for a couple of days by the time I'd gotten there. While waiting to board the ship, I bumped into an old friend from the RAF, Warren Lawson, he was just standing there with his suitcase. When he saw me, he came over and said, 'Gardie boy, I want to go England, but me have no money for ticket.' I wanted to help him, but I didn't know how. I'd have even paid for his if I could, but I had no money left over.

As we were talking, a crew member came onto the deck. The crowd fell silent as the man started to call out the names of people who were allowed to board the ship. To my surprise my name was called out. What I did not know at the time was that my name had already been put down on the passenger list. Lynn had told her housemate that I had the money for a ticket and was on my way to the docks, so he made sure that my name was on the list.

Before I boarded, I needed to help Warren. We noticed that there was a lot of coming and going from the ship, with passengers from the other islands coming down to the docks and just having a walkabout. We got talking to some Trinidadians and between us we were able to get a pass for Lawson. One of the Trinidadians would stay on board so that Lawson could use his pass. We weren't the only ones who had this idea.

Chapter Ten

There were a few more stops on the way to England. Two days in Havana, then onto Mexico before stopping in Bermuda for five days. When the ship docked at Mexico it picked up some Polish nationals who had been displaced during the war and were returning to Poland. It was mainly women and children and a few older people.

Five days in Bermuda was five days too long. Don't get me wrong, England wasn't a racism-free paradise, but I did find most of the people tolerant and friendly. Yes, I'd been given the odd look, sometimes words were exchanged and sometimes it went further, but it didn't compare to the racism of Bermuda.

Bermuda at the time had its own form of apartheid. There were separate entrances to buildings, one for whites and one for coloureds, it was something we had not seen before. Being Jamaican, I, along with my brother Gladstone and friends Zane and Gaynor, took no notice of signs and even had a picnic in a park that we were not supposed to enter. Luckily no one in authority spotted us or we may have been in trouble. A white man did come to tell us that we couldn't sit in the park. With a couple of choice words he was told what to do with himself.

On the last night in Bermuda there was a dance and this was the only time that the men on the ship were able to mix with the females who were on board the *Windrush*, with the male passengers occupying the cabins below deck and the females taking the upper cabins. Even when on deck there was no mixing of sexes, with areas cordoned off from each other by the ship's crew. The West Indian ladies were mostly nurses going to the UK to look for work in the newly formed NHS.

Though we'd managed to get Lawson on the ship, it was not until later in the voyage that I found there were quite a few stowaways on the ship. Nobody really knows for sure how many, every now and again the ship's crew would do a headcount because they knew that there were stowaways on board, but we all worked together to keep the stowaways hidden.

We developed a system, hiding them in toilets, or in lifeboats, or some just walking around the ship. We would share our food with them, when it came to sleeping, those of us who had bunks would let the stowaways use them while we walked around the deck. On arriving in England some were caught when the ship docked because they didn't have the correct paperwork and ended up in court, as far as I am aware some were given short jail sentences, but nobody was deported.

There was one female stowaway, Evelyn Wauchope, who was found a few days into the journey. I say 'found', but I believe she gave herself up, as it was too cold for her outside at night. I don't blame her. Anyway the men decided to have a whip round to pay for her passage. One of the main collectors of the money was one of the male stowaways, hiding in plain sight.

I enjoyed the journey on the HMT *Empire Windrush*, it was a happy ship. Just people lying about on the deck of the ship and all of us hoping for a good life in the UK, it was a bit like a holiday. There was no organised entertainment that I can remember, but there was quite a bit of gambling, with dice, card games and dominoes. No one had much money, so we gambled for cigarettes.

They could be used as currency on the ship, but more than that it was just a way to pass the time. I still wasn't smoking. Honestly, smoking has always disgusted me since I quit. It was hard to avoid the smoke emitted by so many smokers confined to one ship, but it was a massive ship and there was always space to walk around. Quite a few of us would jog around the deck for exercise. I also took walks all the time, sometimes just to clear my head, sometimes in search of a game. If you saw an empty space at a card school you would just sit down and join in.

Thanks to calypso artists Lord Kitchener and Lord Beginner there was always music on the ship. Lord Kitchener could make a song from any sound, the humming of the engine, someone just banging on the ship's safety rail or someone just tapping their feet, to the sound of domino players banging down their dominos.

There was also another singer on the ship, Harold Phillips. He later moved to Liverpool and became known as Lord Woodbine. He was the first mentor of a band he promoted, they were so close that the band was occasionally known as 'Woodbine's Boys', but most people know them as the Beatles. Woodbine convinced the Beatles to add a drummer and he even performed on the same stage as the Beatles in Hamburg.

There was also a keen entrepreneurial spirit on the ship. No one better represented this spirit than Kennedy, a friend of mine. Somehow Kennedy had managed to get hold of tins of peaches and prunes. He would go around the ship selling slices of the fruits for a penny or two, depending on how well he knew you. 'Gardie boy,' he would say when he saw me. 'Come have a slice of peach,' and I would always get a free slice.

As the ship neared Tilbury, excitement and anticipation started to build up among the passengers, but we were not fully aware of members of Parliament's attempts to refuse landing permission for the ship. They were not happy that so many West Indians were coming to make England their home. On the way up the Thames, the *Windrush* was escorted by HMS *Sheffield*, which may have been waiting to turn the ship around, if ordered too. As the ship neared port a couple of men jumped ship and swam to shore, as other passengers ran to the side of the ship to see what was happening, there were so many men on that side of the ship, that the captain had to issue a warning and asked everyone to disperse and move away from that side of the ship because it was starting to list.

For most of the men onboard the ship, including me, the idea was to stay in England for about five years, hopefully find a good job, make some money, and return home to the West Indies. I was 22 at the time, I didn't understand how hard it is to make a five year plan, I guess then five years seemed inordinately long. So why couldn't I anticipate how much my life would change in that time? I would be a different man at 27 than I was at 22.

On 21 June, the ship was anchored just outside Tilbury, waiting for permission to dock. Permission was eventually granted, and the *Empire Windrush* docked on 22 June. TV cameras and reporters from the daily papers were waiting, and some of the passengers were interviewed, including Lord Kitchener, who sang his now famous song, 'London is the place for me.'

In all the media footage I have watched there are no images of me or Gladstone, the reason being, we were helping my friend Warren and another stowaway, Cliff Hall, he was also an ex-RAF man, to disembark safely.

Chapter Eleven

While most of the men on board had set their mind on staying in London, some of the ex-RAF men wanted to go back near to where they had been stationed. Like me they were eager to re-acquaint themselves with the young women they'd left behind. I never took to London anyway; even without the girls, Leeds made sense to me. Of course, I hadn't forgotten about them.

We got the stowaways off the ship the same way we got them on the ship, with people passing passes back and forth. As we disembarked, the ex-RAF men were approached by RAF officers. They wanted us to rejoin the force, and implied we'd be looking at promotions if we did. However, re-enlisting had been a daily topic of discussion on the ship. Due to the number of servicemen returning to the UK, promotion was out of the question. The RAF officers were massaging the truth to get us to sign up again, but we weren't having it.

We politely rejected the RAF officials on the docks, told them our plans, and we were issued with travel passes. I was determined to get back to Leeds and though I'd enjoyed my time serving, I was done with the RAF. I knew people in Leeds and hopefully I'd find a place to stay and then find employment. We caught the train to Fenchurch Street station, then made our way across London to Kings Cross, where we caught the first train we could to Leeds. It was me, Gladstone, Warren Lawson, and Cliff Hall, who I met on the ship.

Cliff would later move to Liverpool and form part of a successful folk group, The Spinners, who had a few chart hits in the '60s. He also married one of the Scottish girls I mentioned earlier who had been living in Greenbanks hostel. Her name was Janet and she was also a friend of Florence.

On arrival at Leeds station, we had a bit of a shock. The local newspaper *The Yorkshire Evening Post* had the headline, 'FIVE JAMAICANS CHARGED IN LEEDS'. So, as we got off the train, we received some strange looks.

There are conflicting stories to exactly what happened on the night of 21 June in the Hyde Park area of Leeds. The newspaper said that five Jamaicans were involved in the trouble, but I heard a different story through the grapevine. In that story, only one of the Jamaicans was involved in the fight, a guy called Johnny Johnson (Herbert Alexander Johnson). The other Jamaicans, Clovis Alexander Lewis, Hugh Percival Young, Fredrick E Williams and Thomas Eccleston, turned up at the incident just as the police arrived, but the police proceeded to arrest all of them.

The story goes that Johnny was renting a room in a house in the Hyde Park area and his white landlady had twin girls. Johnny started to go out with one of them. A couple of local lads were not happy about this 'race-mixing' and threatened Johnny. On the night in question, it was the girls' birthday and Johnny had taken them both out dancing. On their way back home, they were stopped by two lads, who then attacked Johnny.

One of the girls ran to tell her mother and the other went to the house of the other Jamaicans. In the meantime, according to Johnny, who was a big lad, as the two white youths went for him, he managed to get hold of both of them and smashed their heads together. They both went down. Unfortunately for Johnny, a police car was nearby. According to the other Jamaicans, the police drove past them as they were running up the road to help their friend.

As they arrived at the scene the police were helping the two lads, and had already arrested Johnny. For good measure they arrested the four gentlemen who had just shown up. The two Englishmen were taken to the hospital with cuts and bruises. One of the men had a suspected skull fracture.

When it came to court the Jamaicans were found not guilty of causing grievous bodily harm to the two men, but guilty of assault and were bound over for twelve months. Perhaps this version wasn't accurate. I'm sure there were some exaggerations and confabulations in the story, rumours always get distorted, but on the whole, I believe the story. It wouldn't be the last time I heard of black men being treated unfairly by the police.

My brother, Warren, Cliff and I had to find accommodation on the night of our arrival in Leeds. Thanks to the loan from Papa to pay for my journey, I made sure that I had enough money left over to pay for rent, providing that we could find a place to stay. We first travelled to the Greenbanks hostel, where I had stayed during my engineering course. I assumed we'd have no problem staying there again.

On arrival at the hostel, we were told that no more West Indians would be accommodated there because of trouble with some men who had stayed there after I had left in 1947. We then tried some other places where I thought that we could get a room but were rejected again. This time we were told it was different than last time because we were no longer in uniform, it made things awkward. Also 'what would the neighbours say?' I didn't really care what the neighbours might say, but evidently the landlords did. This was a common theme, the landlords and estate agents would tell us they personally didn't mind us, but due to neighbours, housing prices, and potential violence from racists, they couldn't rent to us.

As we were looking for places to stay, we saw the signs in some of the windows, 'NO IRISH, NO BLACKS, NO DOGS'. We found it hard to get our heads around those signs. Just a few years ago we were being welcomed by these people, now we couldn't even find a place to sleep. Worrying never solved anything though, the priority was to find a place to sleep that night.

We persevered and eventually managed to find a bed and breakfast that first night. I called on a friend of mine from the RAF who had decided to stay in Leeds. I asked him for some help, guessing he'd been in similar situations while staying in Leeds. Unfortunately I was right, he'd been facing these same difficulties since he'd left the RAF. He was happy to help and told us about a house.

Those first few weeks back in the UK, my friends and I moved accommodation a few times, it was always by word of mouth that we found out about a place to stay, sometimes there could be two, three or four of us to a room. A couple of times I even slept in a chair, occasionally on the floor. This was fine, the men I was sharing the rooms with were like brothers, we had to be like brothers back then. We had to support each other.

In August 1948, a few weeks after our arrival in the UK, the Olympic games were being held at the White City Stadium in London. The Jamaican 400m runner Arthur Wint and another Jamaican Herb Mckenley made it to the final of the 400 metres. I knew Arthur Wint personally, he had been a Flight Lieutenant in the RAF. I met him in one of the clubs when I was with Flight Sergeant Johnny Burke.

So we huddled around the radio in the lodging house that we were staying in to listen to the race. As the runners rounded the last bend up against the USA runner Mal Whitfield, we were cheering on the Jamaican runners. We must have been making too much noise because the landlady walked in the room and turned off the radio before the runners had crossed the finishing line. Her excuse was that the radio was overheating and could catch fire. We were certainly not pleased, but could not say anything, we couldn't afford to get kicked out. We found out the next day that the Jamaicans had secured 1st and 2nd with Arthur taking gold.

It was then that I made a mental note to buy a house as soon as I could. Dealing with landlords and estate agents was an absolute nightmare and in those early days our situation felt so precarious. We couldn't even ask to listen to the radio without worrying about being on the streets.

But I digress, Arthur Wint would later got into politics and eventually became Jamaican High Commissioner in 1974, I would go down to London to meet up with him. It wasn't often, but it was as much as we both could manage, so it was enough. We didn't talk all the time, having our own lives, but we were close and I'm glad to say that he was my friend.

Of course, before I could even think about buying a house, I needed a job. Our second day back in Leeds, we all went to the labour exchange. This became a daily ritual for me. And every day, as soon as I walked into the office, the man on the desk would look up and say, 'Sorry son, nothing for you today'. After about three weeks of this, I had almost no money left. These were tough times for us all, I couldn't borrow from my friends, they were in the same boat as me. They didn't have jobs and were down to their last shillings too.

I was actually thinking about re-joining the RAF. We'd left Jamaica for Leeds to find jobs. It was especially frustrating that there were jobs available, just not for us. I understood why the man at the labour exchange refused me every day, but nevertheless I persisted. Every day I would go there, just to try. One day I walked out, perhaps I looked particularly dejected that day, there's only so much rejection a man can stand.

There was a gentleman stood by the door, he stopped me. 'Are you looking for work?' he said.

'Yes,' I answered. I wanted to be cool, nonchalant maybe, but I was grinning from ear to ear.

'Where are you from, son?'

'Jamaica, I just moved to Leeds, but I lived here for a while when I was serving in the RAF.'

He nodded. 'I see. What did you do in the RAF? What experience do you have?'

'I was a motor mechanic. Actually I first came to Leeds to do a six-month engineering training course.' There's a word for this, these happy accidents that almost seem like miracles to you, serendipity. I was getting desperate and dejected, if I hadn't joined the RAF I'd have jumped on whatever job I could get if one became available to me. Now I didn't need to, now the job that I wanted and was qualified for was calling to me.

'Can you strip an engine?' He asked me.

'Of course I can. It's putting it back together again which is the problem.' We laughed about this. The man had a small engineering workshop and he must have been impressed because he offered me a job on the spot. We got in his car and he took me to his workshop. That was my first job as a civilian in England, stripping tank engines for this gentlemen at his small company, Commercial Engineers. He asked me if I knew any other men looking for a job, so I was able to get my brother and a couple of friends jobs as well.

I was daydreaming one day while on the job, factory work can become so monotonous. All of a sudden, I heard Charlie Dawkins shout, 'Ford! Duck!' I sprang out of my daydream and did what I was told. The tank engine being carried on the overhead crane shot over my head, so close I felt the breeze. If I hadn't ducked, it would have smashed my head open like an egg. The moral of the story is to always help your friends when you can. It will save your life one day.

These were still hard times and overall we still found it hard to feel welcome in this city that we'd chosen as our new home. Though we had jobs now, we were still looking for a place to call our own. A few weeks after the incident over the radio, I became acquainted with a West Indian man named Basil Blackwood. Basil told me about a house on Clarendon Place, owned by a man called Robbie, who was renting rooms to West Indians. Gladstone, Lawson, and I went to enquire and were able to get a room, Cliff had decided to go his own way. There were already some West Indians living in the house, Marcus, Hyman, Stewart, Frank Kelly, and Charlie Dawkins. I remember thinking there were enough West Indians to form a cricket team, so we decided to create one.

We moved in soon after. One night when we were all asleep there was all this banging and shouting. Someone angrily knocking on my bedroom door, trying to get in. I jumped out of bed and Tommy Tomlinson, who I was sharing the room with at this time, also jumped up. We had no idea what was happening. Though we'd just woken up, we were alert and on edge, wondering who was trying to break in.

Our door wasn't built to withstand this mysterious intruder. It gave way soon enough, but we were ready by then. As soon as the man came through the door I grabbed him. In my post-sleep state I didn't have the time to reason, just to act. I hit the man and Tommy helped me. Then I heard someone shouting out, 'Police, this is a raid' as lights turned on. We watched policemen fill the room, I'd have rather it been a burglar honestly. We calmed down, because we had to, and let them subdue us. They got the other men from their rooms and got us all together in the kitchen.

By this time Robbie, the owner, who lived in the top flat had come down to see what all the commotion was. A police sergeant came into the room and explained that there had been a complaint from one of the neighbours regarding some kind of noisy disturbance at the house. This took us all by surprise because at the time of the so-called disturbance we were all in bed.

I'd have thought the fact that there was no noise when the police came would have helped them realise that, but no luck. Another man may have pointed out that the only people disturbing the peace at the dead of night were the police, but I was a smarter man than that. I just wanted to go back to bed. After taking statements from us all the sergeant decided that there was no need to take the matter any further and concluded that it must have been one of the neighbours out to cause trouble.

It was nice living with so many of my close friends, but it was a little crowded. It also made it difficult to entertain women. Logistically it was hard enough, as we were at least two to a room, but the landlord had told us that we would not be allowed to entertain young ladies in the rooms. That was a problem for me.

Again my mind turned to buying a house. My job was going smoothly. I was a hard worker and this was a very nice job for my first year in the UK. The tank engines that I was helping to strip were being shipped to Kuwait. I was put in charge of wiring the engines. It always pleased me when an engine started up for the first time after I'd worked on it. One day some men came over from Kuwait to see how things were going, and they were very pleased at the work we were doing. There was talk of some of us being offered jobs to go work over in Kuwait. Most of my friends had the same mentality as me, they'd come to England to make money, some of them were even sending what they could back home. If they could make more in another country, they'd follow the money.

One of the men from Kuwait came to see me and asked if I had any engineering qualifications, like an apprenticeship or City and Guilds.

'I have nothing like that.' I said.

'That's a pity. Without qualifications we will not be able to offer you any type of employment,' he said and walked off. With hindsight, I should have thought about going to night school to try and get some qualifications, but at this point I wasn't thinking of education or the next step, I was taking the time to enjoy myself in this city.

Now that I had a place and a job, enjoyment was my chief concern. We all enjoyed dancing and nights at the Mecca were a regular fixture again. I was excited to see Florence, Margaret and Norma again. Florence and I had always been a contradiction, our relationship was intense in some ways, but also very casual. She didn't know I was back, but even if I had told her I was coming back, I wouldn't have expected her to wait for me, nor would I have wanted that.

I was young, and having left the RAF, I felt like a weight had been lifted off my shoulders, I felt freer than I had in a while. I didn't want to settle down, perhaps that's why I hadn't sought out the girls. I wanted to enjoy myself in Leeds as a young man. I was a bit of a player, to be honest. Indeed, I was always honest about my intentions with the women I encountered. Nevertheless, my brother Gladstone had some misgivings with my lifestyle.

Left to right, Gibbs, unknown man, Jupiter, me and Butler posing with a Spitfire

Dennis (left) and I, 1945

ROYAL AIR FORCE. R.A.F. Form 1383

DEFICIENCIES OF KIT.

Number... 413306 ... Rank... LAC.

Name... GARDNER. A.D.

Trade... M.T.M.

Certified that the Kit of the above-named airman is deficient of the items detailed overleaf. The deficiencies arose owing to, or at,

Kitting on enlistment. (IV. No....................refers.)
Promotion
Posting to....................
Remustering
Increase in scale authorised by....................

P.O.R. No....................refers. (P.O.R. is not required for deficiencies on kitting on enlistment).

Date of Issue
and Unit Stamp.

P/G No. 39 M.U.

COLERNE,

WILTS.

Signature.................... F/S
Senior Equipment Officer.

This Form must be taken care of and surrendered by the airman named hereon when all deficient items have been issued to him. The airman will be charged for any deficiencies discovered in his kit if he fails to produce this form unless there are sufficient grounds for write-off against the public.

*15948—5057) Wt. 51202—4190 320M 2/45 T.S. 700

Deficiency Card

Section	Reference No.	ITEM	Quantity	Issued on EV.
22D	459	SHOES Canvas	One	
22F	432	Coats Great.	One	
22B	3	Braces.	One	
22B	81	Cap Comforter	One	
22B	19	Dressing Field	One	
22B	25	Holdall	One	
23	1	Bags Ration	One	
One	Complete set of Webbing Equipment			

DEFICIENT ITEMS. (All entries are to be made in ink.)

Unused lines are to be struck through by the Issuing Officer.

Required Items

R.A.F. FORM 1394.

SC/V12
EWR 60

ROYAL AIR FORCE.

BRIEF STATEMENT OF SERVICE AND CERTIFICATE OF DISCHARGE OF

The corner of this certificate to be cut off if the airman/airwoman is discharged with a "bad" character, or with disgrace or if specially directed by the Air Council.

SURNAME... **GARDNER** .... OFFICIAL No... **713306** ......

CHRISTIAN NAMES...... **Alford Dalrymple**

Date of enlistment **17.3.44.** .... Terms of enlistment **Duration of present**

(a) Date reported for regular service **17.3.44.** **emergency.**

(b) Branch of Air Force in which enlisted... **R.A.F.V.R.**... R.A.F. trade on discharge **Motor Transport Mechanic**

Date of discharge... **1st March, 1948.** ...... Rank on discharge **Leading Aircraftsman**

(c) Cause of discharge.. **On termination of engagement under**

(Para. **652** Clause **1** King's Regulations and Air Council Instructions.)

(d) General character (i) during service.. **Very Good** .... (ii) on discharge.. **Very Good**

(e) Degree of trade proficiency :—A.. **Satisfactory** .... B..

Special qualifications..

(f) Medals, Clasps, Decorations, Mentions in Despatches, Special Commendations, etc. { **None** }

DESCRIPTION OF ABOVE-NAMED AIRMAN/AIRWOMAN ON DISCHARGE.

Date of birth ...... **27.2. 1926** .... Marks or scars **1 Scar Right Foot.**

Height.......... **5.** ft. **81/2** ins.

Complexion **Dark**

Colour of eyes........ **Brown** .... Colour of hair...... **Black**

Airman's or airwoman's signature ....

(g) Brief statement of any special aptitudes or qualities or any special types of employment for which recommended :—

General Character Good. His work as a Mechanic is above average under supervision, but has tendency to lose interest in his work without that supervision.

ROYAL AIR FORCE
ACCOUNTS UNIT.

Unit
Date
Stamp **DEC 20 1947**
**BADOES. JAMAICA.
BRITISH WEST INDIES.**

(Signed) .... **W/CMDR.**

Commanding **No. 39 M.U.R.A.F. COLERNE, WILTS.**
Royal Air Force.

Attention is directed to Notes (a) to (g) on reverse.

My Discharge Document

Grandma and Patricia

Gan-Gan

My parents

Players and families on their way to cricket

Howard and I at a cricket match May 1953

Taking a break between innings

Champions of inter-departmental cricket competition at Barnbow works. Photo: 1957/58

Receiving my first-aider certificate

Getting ready for a night out, Noel Edwards (Sabu) and I with friends.

Gladstone and Ruth

Jean and I

Me outside Clarendon Place

20 Clarendon Place today

23 Brudenell Mount, our family home.

23 Brudenell Mount today

Cynthia, Howard and Joseph outside Regent Terrace

21 Regent Terrace today

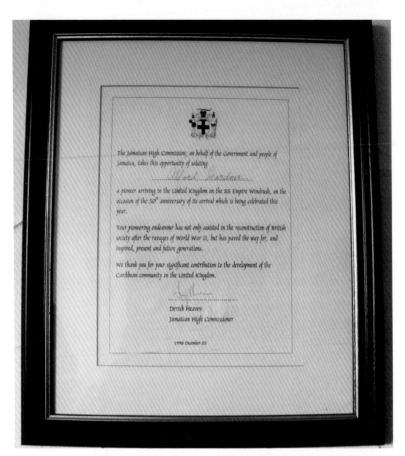

An award from the Jamaican High Commission

Banner and plaque in Tilbury Dock Terminal

Me at the National Windrush Monument at Waterloo Station

Windrush Awards 2018

Jim and Ruth Grover, Howard and I at the gallery@oxo

Paula and I with an advert for the gallery@oxo exhibition

Weekes Baptiste and I on stage Fairfield Hall, Croydon

Susan Pitter and I

Howard, Baroness Floella Benjamin and I

Outside No. 10

Baroness Floella Benjamin and I

Me in the shirt I presented to the NLJ

Mr John Holder and I

Mr Allan Charles Wilmot and I

John Richards and I in conversation

Mr Roper and I presenting the Eulogy book to Leeds City Council leader Mrs Judith Blake

Me visiting the Jamaican rugby team at Headingley

Gladstone was more religious than me and strictly monogamous. He did not approve of the way I was behaving and of my attitude to the fairer sex. We weren't the type to have a bad argument about my behaviour, even a real discussion about it wasn't on the table. There were passive-aggressive comments and questions here and there, but nothing major. I noted his concern and ignored it, seeing it as none of his business.

One night while I was in the Mecca, dancing the night away, I saw Florence. Johnny Johnson had already told me that she had started to see someone a few weeks after I had returned home, so it wasn't a shock to me when I saw her with another man. She thought I would never come back.

'Ford? Fordie, is that you?' Florence said, coming closer to me, not quite believing it. It's easy to mistake one man for another in the dark of the mecca hall, but she got so close to me that I didn't even need to answer. She had moved on, but when she saw me, a strong mix of emotions all came to a head at once and she burst into tears. I hugged her, for no reason other than to comfort an old friend.

Her new man saw all of this. He bounded over to me, quicker than Florence had run to me and started to shout at me.

'How dare you?' He shouted and before I could answer and tell him that I had not dared to do anything with Florence, he continued to rant and rave at me. His fists were still by his side, but they were clenched and I've been in enough bars and clubs to recognise a fight before it breaks out. Florence was still crying in my arms at the time, this was surely only enraging him more.

He kept on at it. Though he was shouting at me, it was more like he was having a very loud, animated conversation with himself, working himself up so he could hit me. I managed to calm him down by explaining that I had also moved on, Florence and I were now just friends. A few weeks after that meeting Florence moved back home to Scotland. I never saw or heard from her again.

I kept on enjoying myself as a young man in Leeds, but my living situation was getting to me. Even if I was allowed to bring girls back home, I had about ten people living with me, I didn't even have a room to myself. So towards the end of 1949, five of us decided to buy a house. Along with Warren Lawson, Lloyd Tomlinson, (no relation to Tommy Tomlinson), Vince Stewart, and Clarence Sullivan, we purchased a large house for £500 on Regent Terrace, in the Hyde Park area of Leeds. We each had our own room, which was a luxury after having to share a room, a few times I remember eight of us staying in one room.

The house itself was a large Victorian house, with a huge entrance lobby and a wide sweeping staircase and two reception rooms. The bedrooms were over the two top floors. The kitchen was down in the basement, and it took up the whole floor. It was near Woodhouse Moor, a large park area where we would go to practice cricket and play football. The park is close to the now famous and listed building The Hyde Park Picture House.

There were four pubs, the Little Park, the Hyde Park, the Royal Park, and the Newlands, all within walking distance. The church All Hallows opposite the house, the old church burnt down in 1970, and a new one was built in its place in 1974. The house is still there and is now used for student accommodation. The Newlands and Little Park pubs are no longer there but the other two are still going. We would often call in the Newlands, or sometimes the Royal Park for a drink before heading out to Mecca.

I went to the pub a lot while in the RAF because it was all there was to do and all that my friends ever did. Not that I didn't like pubs or alcohol, just that there were things I'd rather be doing. Things I'd rather spend my money on. So at this time of my life, I was not a regular pub man. Since we'd left the RAF a lot of things had changed, some of the local population didn't like to see us in the pubs now that we were no longer wearing a uniform.

You could tell as soon as you walked into a pub if you were welcome or not, just by looking at the faces of the locals. Sometimes you could feel the eyes of the whole pub on you, some people nervously whispering about you, others talking about your presence but not being so polite as to whisper. If you had a bad feeling about a place, the best thing to do was get out as soon as possible. If there was any trouble, the only people who would be arrested would be the black men, no matter who started it.

I've never liked to focus on the negatives of life though, especially when they were out of my control. I couldn't change the hearts and minds of these people, but I didn't have to seek out their company. Anyway there was a lot going well for me. I had a house and I had a good job. The pub wasn't important to me then, I had other forms of entertainment.

Chapter Twelve

Many nights and weekends were spent hard at work, but when I wasn't working those long nights and weekends were taken up with dancing at the Mecca, gambling, playing cards, and betting on the horses. As soon as we were paid, we would meet at someone's house to play poker, quite often one could lose all our wages in one session. Those who had lost all their money would sometimes try to beg for loans from the winners, but they were always knocked back, it was one of those things, if you lose, tough.

I believe that failure was a good teacher in gambling, no one made a habit of losing their paycheck. Thankfully that never happened to me. I always made sure that my money went on food and clothing before any bets or stakes were made. My stake money was what was left after the bills had been paid.

There were three formats we would play, no matter if it was cards or dominoes, there was the penny game, the shilling game and the pound game. Most of us would start with the penny game, hoping to make enough money to progress to the shilling game. If you managed to get to the pound game you knew that you were in the money, but once you started to lose in the pound game, the money would disappear in a flash.

Now I know that I said if you lost your money, then it was tough, but usually you could go to someone that trusted you and who knew that they would get their money back. At first you would ask for a pound to join the pound game, more than likely they would say no, you would then ask for a shilling to join the shilling game, the answer would still be no, and you eventually settled on a penny. From that penny you'd hopefully progress to the pound game and win it all back. This rarely happened, and more often than not you'd lose it all again.

It was not just the West Indians from Leeds who played in these card schools, there was also a group of West Indians who would come over from Manchester to play. I was never a great poker player and would lose more than I'd win. One night after losing quite heavily, a friend took me to one side and told me that the guys from Manchester had been cheating. I did not believe him until he showed me how they were manipulating the cards. I didn't make a fuss about it, but it was the last time I played poker.

I even visited a casino a couple of times. I went one night after winning £50 at bingo, because my luck was in. It seemed I'd used up all my luck for that night though. I changed £20 into chips and watched them vanish in the blink of an eye. I went a few more times with friends, I lost a bit of money, hesitant to play after my first experience. I watched some of them lose a lot of money and chase their losses, I'd never seen anything like it. It was like these men were possessed, I couldn't get them to stop or see sense. That was my last time in the casino.

What I really loved to gamble on in those days was the horses. A few of the lads would organise trips to the racetracks in and around Yorkshire, places like York, Wetherby, Doncaster, and Ripon. They were excellent days out, it was not about just winning money, but that helped, it was about enjoying the occasion with your closest friends. In my time I have probably bet on everything.

There was also sport. Along with Charlie Dawkins, my housemates at Regent Terrace and some more of our friends, we formed a cricket club. This was in 1948 not long after I had arrived in Leeds. Some of the other guys had remained in Leeds after being demobbed. We knew it was a way to get to know the English people and being in Yorkshire with its rich heritage in the sport, it was a good way to go about it.

The first thing we had to do was to obtain some cricket gear. We went to a local sports store owned by Herbert Sutcliffe, the Yorkshire and England opening batsman. We agreed to buy some equipment on hire purchase, but when we went to pick it up, someone in higher management had vetoed the sale, no reason was given.

I actually met Mr Sutcliffe a few years later at a cricket match, the team was just starting to make a name for ourselves. He asked me why we didn't buy our equipment from his store and that he would give us a discount if we went there. I told him we had tried, but we had been knocked back by someone in higher management. He told me that he was not aware of that incident but would try and find out what happened, and that he would make sure that something like that would not happen in his store again. He seemed genuine, but I was stubborn. After that first incident I wouldn't shop at his store, I know that some of the other guys did go there to buy their kit.

After being unable to buy the kit, we managed to beg and borrow some pads, bats, balls, and wickets and we started to practise. No matter where we went to practise, the police would come along and stop us from playing. Some of these places were public parks, so we could not understand the problem. We eventually started to practise on Woodhouse Moor, which was not too far from Clarendon Place. The police didn't bother us there, now we just had the problem of finding other teams to play.

In that first year we only managed to play two matches, and then about five the year after. By the third year, 1950, we were starting to become known and other teams were starting to invite us to their ground to play against them. Luckily, being in Yorkshire there were a lot of established clubs and teams like Kirkstall Liberal Working Men's club and Kirkstall Educational, another well-known club in Leeds at the time, were happy to play against us newcomers.

In the early days of the Caribbean Cricket Club, or CCC as we came to be known as, we could not always get eleven players. Players from the opposing team would sometimes help us to make up the team. Sometimes, some of the West Indians who lived over in Manchester (when not cheating at cards) would occasionally come over to Leeds to play cricket with us.

It was now a question of who was good at batting, bowling, and fielding, after a few games we found out that we were all good at fielding. I eventually became the wicketkeeper. Charlie Dawkins was a fast bowler and Bill Turnbull an elegant batter. Errol James became our club president. Some, like Clovis Lewis, realised that they weren't cricketers at all. Clovis became our first club secretary and Johnny Johnson became our umpire.

Clovis took his role seriously, he probably sent an invite to any cricket team in and around Yorkshire, and we managed to get games with village teams all across Yorkshire, and sometimes over into Lancashire. To get to a match we would hire a coach, and wives and girlfriends along with children would also attend the match.

On the way back from these matches we would often stop at a country pub for a pint or two, but we could never be sure what kind of reception we would receive at the pub, so a couple of the wives or girlfriends would go into the pub first, just to see the lay of the land. Up until the late '60s, some pubs and especially Working Men's Clubs had a colour bar, so we always had to be careful.

The team eventually got into a league and were soon winning trophies and championships. The team managed to rent Leeds council playing fields on Soldiers Field in Roundhay, then on to Beckett Park in Leeds before moving to their permanent home on Scott Hall Road, Leeds, where the team are still playing to the present day.

Those were the days. I was living the high life, playing cricket on the weekend, then out dancing at night-time, gambling on an evening after work, just what every young man wants. Eventually no matter where I went Norma and Margaret were never far away, as with Florence I'd met them both again in the Mecca, but this was a much happier reunion. It became the three of us out together most of the time. I was often seen walking around the streets with a girl on each arm, my friends would shout out things like 'Gardie boy, I don't know how you do it' or words to that effect.

But it's a universal law of life that nothing stays the same forever. I began to see life slowly change. Norma and I began to bond with each other as surely and as helplessly as falling in love always seems to happen. Margaret seemed to slowly drift away from us. She'd been hinting that Norma had more serious feelings for me and eventually she just told me that Norma was more in love with me than she was.

Norma wanted kids, as did I. Margaret didn't. There are a million facts that could have supported Norma and I falling for each other and a million facts that got in the way, but in the end it's not the facts that matter. It's just the feelings you both have and I had all the feelings for Norma. We would always love Margaret, but I think she felt like a third wheel, and we saw less and less of her.

Meanwhile, the job stripping tank engines was coming to an end, Charlie Dawkins and I were advised that if we wanted to continue to work in engineering, we would need to join the union (the AUEW) and that I would only be able to obtain semi-skilled employment, because I had not done a recognised engineering apprenticeship. At that time the majority of UK factories operated a closed shop, which meant you had to be in a union before you could be employed.

We attended the local AUEW (Amalgamated Union of Engineering Workers) meeting and as we walked in, the president said, 'What are you two doing here?' and tried to throw us out.

Old Fred was a staunch union man who I worked with at Commercial Engineering. He had taken us under his wing, but even if we'd never met him before, I don't think his principles would have allowed him to stay silent.

'They have come to join the union,' Old Fred said sternly.

'They need a job to join this union,' the president replied not knowing that we already had employment. Once he learned that, he added some caveats. 'And they need to be proposed and seconded,' he was really having a go at us. The man sat next to him had to calm him down. I'll never understand how the colour of my skin can make these people so mad.

One of the men in the meeting stood up and proposed us. The vice-president of the union branch seconded us, a vote was taken and passed. So, Charlie and I were now in the union, this paved the way for other West Indians to join the union, hopefully it would make it easier for us to find employment. True democracy at work.

That job finished soon enough, due to the lack of work, but it was easy to find work then. I'd seen a lot of people come and go at Commercial Engineers. With the war not long over, orders for work in the factories were at a premium. The thing about a peak is that it's all downhill from there. You'd be hired as a factory needed more men to fill a job and then you'd be canned just as easily. Redundancies were always on the cards, and it was last man in - first man out at the time, but there always seemed to be a vacancy somewhere. You could always find work, but you could lose it just as fast, they'd find a replacement tomorrow if they needed it.

I went on to work at one of the larger companies in Leeds, Yorkshire Copperworks. What I realised early on was that I, along with my fellow West Indians, had to make sure the components we were producing had to be as good as, if not better than, the person working alongside us. Being black, if there was any flaw in our work, we could be out the door. I knew this and I tried to make myself irreplaceable at work. I worked harder and smarter than everyone else. The components I produced were impeccable and I made them faster too. I took every shift going. I played hard, but I always worked the hardest.

When I worked at Yorkshire Copperworks I would travel there on a bike, setting off from Clarendon Place with just enough time to clock in.

One evening just as it was just starting to get dark, I had stopped at a set of lights when a police car pulled up beside me. A young policeman got out of his car and told me that I should not be riding the bike because it had no lights.

'It has lights,' I said, pointing to a reflector and lights on the back and front.

'Not good enough.' The officer said, shaking his head. Then he said, very slowly, 'They should be lit so that people can see them.'

I have respect for the law and every man has to make a living, but no one has the right to talk down to me. However, all my encounters with the police since returning to Leeds had been unpleasant and Leeds was relatively good. A lot of my friends had moved to London when they came to England, the stories I was hearing about the police in London were enough to give me nightmares. I'd made the right choice coming to Leeds.

All this is to say is that I knew it wasn't a bright idea to talk back to the police. This was true at the best of times, in the best circumstances, it's not right, it's just how it is. That's how power works. Being black and alone in the starless night with only this officer, who had been itching to stop me, for company, this wasn't the best of times. You could be forgiven for thinking I tried to de-escalate things, but that's not my style.

Things were starting to become heated when another police car pulled up and a sergeant got out of the car. 'What's going on here?' he asked us.

'He doesn't have a light on his bike and he's been giving me lip about it, sarge.' The young officer said.

The sergeant came over and had a look at the bike, shook his head and called the young officer over. 'Have you never seen a dynamo on a bike before? If you had not been so eager to question him, you would have seen the lights on the bike light up as soon as he started to peddle away,' he said. Then he turned to me, 'On your way son.'

I set off to work leaving a red-faced policeman being told off by his sergeant. So, as you can imagine, I was riding high. I had a good job,

I worked hard and, by god, I played hard. I was loving life, but not everyone loved how I was living. Gladstone had made it known how he disagreed with my lifestyle, and I, in my own way, had made it known that I didn't care what he thought. I continued to have my fun in Leeds. There was never a big argument, some kind of blow out, he never told me off, I never told him off, I just came home from work one day and there he wasn't.

I knocked on his door to see if he wanted to play cards and he didn't answer. I went in and his room was bare, as if he had been burgled by an extremely thorough man. I couldn't wrap my head around it.

'He's gone.' Warren told me.

I didn't speak. I didn't know what to say. All the questions that first came to mind sounded stupid. *Why? Why wouldn't he say something?* Broadly I knew why, better than Warren anyway. He lived with us and he saw how we were with each other, but he could never understand our relationship the way we knew it. It hurt that he left, but it hurt more that it was because of me. He was fed up of my behaviour, fed up of trying to change me. My brother had packed up and left without saying goodbye, he didn't even leave a note. I try not to take things personally, but I had to wonder where everything went wrong. How do you fix something when neither party has any regrets about their behaviour? Gladstone was always more religious than me, but I wonder how much his views on monogamy were related to my father's extramarital affair that led to his birth? It was too late to regret and I didn't see it all so clearly then as I do now.

'Where did he go?' I finally asked.

'Manchester, he has a new job other there.'

I went back to my room, I needed to be alone. The same stupid questions tumbled over in my head and I wondered when I'd see my brother again, the only family I had in this place. We didn't call or write to each other that day. Or the next. It was a while before we exchanged a single word.

Chapter Thirteen

It's ironic that things between me and Gladstone had deteriorated so much because in 1950, around Christmas, my relationship with Norma became very serious in a typical way. The thing that all couples hope never happens, happened, Norma was pregnant. I was surprised though I had no right to be. We weren't planning it, but these things happen. I took it in stride. It was the wrong time in my life, and for Norma too, she was only nineteen and training to be a seamstress. The baby wouldn't have much family around. Norma and I weren't married, we weren't living together, it was a mess. So why were we giddy with excitement? Why were we so assured and confident? Wrong time maybe, but the conditions are never perfect. Norma was the one and I knew she'd be a wonderful mother, I couldn't wait to have a baby with her.

Ostensibly my plan was to come to England, make some money, have my fun and return to Jamaica, but I'd forgotten those plans the moment I'd stepped foot in Leeds. I didn't even have enough money to return to Jamaica. I had been working hard and was making a good amount of money by taking every shift I could, but I was spending as much as I made. I never had to borrow and my bills were always paid on time, but once the essentials were sorted, the rest was spent on having fun, which for me at the time was going out dancing with Norma and gambling.

Finding out Norma was pregnant brought me a great sense of focus.

Once I was a bright teenager still in school, I saw my future like the leaves of a palm tree. This leaf was my future as a doctor, following in my mother's footsteps and helping the people of my community. In another future I was an athlete, the runner that my dad could have been. A policeman, a carpenter, a soldier. So much possibility and I was so eager to get going and see what I would go on and be.

In Leeds my future had been confined to one dark tunnel. I was on a singular track, no turns, no forks, no diversions. My life was going only one way, only I couldn't clearly see where it was going. My baby and Norma became my guiding light. I could see my entire future now, unfolding so clearly before me and set in place. It wasn't in Jamaica; it was in Leeds. I had a new home now with Norma and our coming child. Though I'd had other girlfriends, Norma was my first real love. I wanted to do the right thing by her, so I went to ask her father for her hand in marriage.

I had never met her parents before. All I really knew about them was that they lived on the Bramley estate, Norma lived with them. Being Jamaican, an estate to me was a large house with plenty of land. When Norma told me she lived on an estate, I was blown away. I asked her if she was rich or even royal. I'd known her for a while, but her being secretly wealthy came as a shock to me. She threw her head back and laughed sweetly. She said she wasn't rich but didn't explain the joke.

When we arrived at Norma's home, I found out what a council housing estate was. I understood what was so funny. Norma had not told her parents that I was black, she was the type of person who didn't see the need to. I was the first man she had ever introduced to her parents. Norma's mother welcomed me into her home with a big grin on her face and I saw where Norma got her radiance from.

Norma's mother sat me and Norma down in the living room and went to get me a glass of water. While she was gone her husband, Norma's father, entered the room. 'What's he doing here? Get him out of my house,' he said as soon as he saw me.

I didn't expect this reaction, but it wasn't the first time I'd have to leave somewhere because of the colour of my skin. It was the first time, however, that someone had kicked me out of their home because I was black. I'd come with my heart on my sleeve and butterflies in my stomach to look Norma's father in the eye and ask for his blessing, but the man couldn't even tolerate the sight of me with his daughter. It was humiliating.

Norma was even more shocked by her father's attitude to me than I was. To her, it was out of character. Indeed, that was her first encounter with racism. I did not say anything to him. I just stood up and walked out of the house.

I hadn't taken two steps when I heard Norma say, 'If he goes, I'm going too'. She followed me out of the house, slammed the door behind her, and we embraced each other. I'd never seen her cry like this before, a deep pain of sadness and fury. She felt betrayed by her father.

'Don't follow me,' I said.

She looked at me, but struggled to get any words out between her laboured breathing. Eventually she gave up and cried into my shoulder.

I told her, 'You need to stay here. We'll work this out. I don't know how, but we can get through anything together.' I started to cry at this point. I was still living in Clarendon Place at this point, there was no room for Norma there.

Just down the road from her house was a large tree with a bench underneath it. We walked down the street and sat on the bench. We talked for ages, about our plans for that night, for the future, how we could bring a baby into this world. She knew that I had been making plans. I was hoping to move in the near future, so we could live together, just me, her and the baby. We needed a big house though, I wanted a big family. In every conversation about the baby I had with Norma, we got so excited about the future we had before us, together in a big house always full of children's laughter and the patter of their tiny feet. That was what I wanted, but I didn't have the money.

A feeling close to regret began to creep up on me, for all these years I had spent in this country and managed not to have a pound saved. I decided not to waste a second in regret. Kicking myself might have felt good, but it was worthless. Anyway I didn't regret enjoying myself, why punish myself for not seeing the future? The baby was coming. The future was arriving, quicker than I thought it would, but I'd just have to meet it.

We talked about the baby. How scared we were. How nervous we were. How excited we were. I was filled with fear and anxiety, I wasn't ready. Would I be a good father? Yet at the same time I had this certainty, this confidence. I would do anything to provide for and to protect my baby.

We talked for hours on that bench and eventually she agreed to go back home. She told me she talked to her parents when she went back home, but she never told me what was said.

Chapter Fourteen

I was working like a madman at the time, even more than I was before, if that was possible. I wanted to be able to move out as soon as possible. I'd stopped going to the Mecca; that was a younger man's sanctuary. I realised that I had to change my lifestyle, I was to be a father soon. I thought of my own father, who I hadn't seen in a couple of years. I wondered if I could be half as good a father as he was. I wondered if I'd make the same mistakes that he did. We all make mistakes. In avoiding the ones my father made I'm sure I'd make my own, that's life, I guess.

Though I didn't see it as a mistake, I knew I needed to mend my relationship with Gladstone. It was early 1951. Norma was beginning to show. Things were still tense between her and her father. I hadn't seen the man since he'd kicked me out of his house, nor did I want to. I wanted the baby to grow up around family though. I had always wanted to have a big family, like the one I grew up in. Norma wanted the same, when I told her I came from a large family, she immediately said, 'That's what I want as well.' We didn't know how many kids we wanted, but we wanted a lot. What is life without family?

Gladstone and I hadn't spoken or seen each other for nearly nine months. I see the day so clearly in my mind's eye. It was a brisk, but beautiful Friday in Leeds and finding myself with nothing to do and feeling a touch sentimental, I decided to go over to Manchester to see him. My brother was never the most expressive person, but I could tell he was happy to see me. We sat down and we talked and laughed and it felt like old times. I told him I had a baby on the way and he was so happy for me. I think he was proud of me.

Maybe it wasn't the conversation we should have had, no, 'How could you?' or, 'What did you expect?', no accusations, no apologies, we just sunk back to our old habits and routines and by the end of it we knew we were fine. I went back to Leeds and picked up a shift on Saturday.

But no matter how much I scrimped and saved and slaved, I knew I wouldn't be able to afford my own place by the time our baby came. On 5 August 1951, Howard Gardner was born. Norma had moved in with me during her third trimester and left her job as a seamstress at a tailoring company. Having a pregnant woman in such cramped living conditions was not ideal. Living in the house with the other men while having a newborn was worse, but we made do. It was still less cramped than our first months in Leeds. Warren Lawson and his partner Mary and their two children Joseph and Cynthia also lived in the house. But what also helped was that the other men were meeting young ladies and during the day when we men were at work there was a bit of company for each other. Norma would also spend a lot of time making clothes for Howard.

Work moved quickly and so did I. Sometimes I left jobs because of layoffs, sometimes I left because there was more money elsewhere. Around the time that Howard came into our lives, I lost my job at Yorkshire Copperworks. I found work the next day at a company called Taylor Rustless, later called Pland. I was only there a few weeks. The work was the same as anywhere, but the pay was much worse.

I heard about a job at another company, Bellow Machine Tool, they made sewing machines, and I jumped at the chance. It had only been a few weeks, but I've never been a fan of job loyalty for no reason. Pay me better and treat me well, I'll be loyal to you. That wasn't happening at Taylor Rustless, so I'd had an eye on the door as soon as I started working there.

I went to Bellow Machine Tool and called at the gatehouse, but as soon as the gatekeeper saw me, he told me that there were no jobs. Gatekeepers, or commissaires as they were sometimes known, were mostly ex-servicemen who were working for the Royal Corp of Commissionaires. It wasn't a high-level job, but you should have tried telling that to some of these men. They believed that they owned the company and were very particular on who they let through the factory gates, this gatekeeper was no different.

'I've been told about jobs here. There are vacancies.' I said.

'All filled up, I'm afraid.' He smiled.

'Since yesterday? All of them? Really?'

'I'm afraid so.'

'You're lying.'

'Don't you dare call me a liar. How dare you?' He could not believe it. 'The likes of you? You? You!? Get out of here, I've told you, there are no jobs here for *you*.' We'd been getting steadily louder, but he had screamed this at me. My calling out his lie had incensed him and he was red-faced now, huffing and puffing, I was genuinely afraid he would work himself up so much he'd have a heart attack. I was unlikely to get the job if that happened.

A senior staff member walking by heard our unfriendly chat and took control of the situation. Apparently there were jobs available and I could interview immediately. Not sure how the gatekeeper had managed to mix that up. The interview went smoothly, I had a lot of experience and they needed men. I started that same day.

Soon after starting at Bellows, I ran into problems with an inspector. In engineering, inspectors would check that the components being produced were up to standard. This inspector had taken an instant dislike to me and was always trying to find fault with my work.

I remember one particular occasion I had taken my work to be inspected. The man barely looked at it before saying, 'it's not up to standard. I'm afraid you'll have to do it again.'

'My work is always impeccable, James. I know this and you know this. Look at it properly.' I said.

'I've looked at it and you haven't magically fixed it. It's not up to standard.'

'You haven't looked at it, or you'd see that it more than meets the requirements.'

'It doesn't meet *my* requirements.'

I'd had enough of this, and evidently the inspector was tired of this conversation too. He called over the foreman (he did not like me either). The foreman agreed with the inspector, he at least pretended to look it over. I knew there was nothing wrong with my work. I took a lot of pride in the quality of my work, but more importantly this affected how much I would be paid. If it hadn't been up to standard I'd have been the first to admit it, but it was flawless. Neither of them had even bothered to make up a flaw either.

Eventually the senior foreman was called. He checked the item and when he couldn't find a flaw, he asked the inspector and foreman what was wrong with it. I couldn't resist smiling as they hemmed and hawed, unable to be specific about what was wrong with my work. He checked it again, as he couldn't understand what the fuss was about. After triple checking the item, he said that the component was of a good standard and allowed me to carry on with my job, which as you can imagine did not please the other two men.

If it seems that I am just talking about work, it's because all I did was work. Babies are more expensive than either Norma or I knew. I felt a pressure to provide the way my dad did for all of us. Norma never said anything or complained about our state of living. Indeed she got on really well with everyone in the household, especially the women who would keep her company and help with Howard. Mary and her became particularly close.

Though Norma was happy, I wanted to give her everything she deserved. I was making as much or more than any of my friends, but it still wasn't enough. We had a roof over our heads and Norma was happy and the baby was healthy. I've always been one to count my blessings, I was happy, but I needed to make more, so we could get our own place.

In October 1952, we found out that I had one more reason to make more money. We had another on the way. The house would be even more crowded, we'd need even more money with another mouth to feed. Don't let my money worries fool you though, we were delighted we were having another child and we'd be able to provide for it no problem, but I wanted more than that. My vision of children playing and laughing in a big house with Norma and me had only grown stronger, clearer over time. Around this time we decided to get married.

I didn't propose to Norma. I'd planned to after I'd received her father's blessing, but that hadn't gone to plan. Though I didn't ask her father for her hand in marriage, I can imagine how he would have answered. Norma and I just sort of decided to get married one day, it made sense and with a second baby on the way, we were getting pretty serious. We had a small wedding the next weekend, with a few close friends coming down to the registry office with us.

My brother Gladstone couldn't make it down on such short notice, but he sent his regards and a gift for Howard. We would catch up in a few weeks anyway when he came down to Leeds for the first time since he'd left without a word. I was glad we were on speaking terms again, it's good for children to have an uncle. The rest of my siblings were 4,600 miles away.

Chapter Fifteen

My second son Roger was born in May 1953. The house was now beginning to become very crowded, what with children and girl-friends all over the place. I'd saved some money, though not as much as I'd have liked, and Norma and I started house hunting. We set about trying to acquire a council house but found out that it was not that easy for a mixed-race couple to get one. We then looked at renting a private house but that was even harder.

So, we stayed put for a while. It wasn't the end of the world. It was cramped, but I knew we'd miss it all as soon as we left. Norma and Mary were best friends at this point, and our children were like siblings more than friends, growing up side by side. I almost didn't want to take them away from each other, but if I've learnt anything about life, it is that everything ends.

I continued to work like a dog. Any dog knows not to bite the hand that feeds it, but I saw some black men take this idea too far. I didn't tolerate disrespect anywhere, not in my home, not in the streets and not at work. Bellows had no redeeming factor, the racist inspector didn't have the power to make my life hell, but his incompetence was frustrating. On top of that, the pay was average there. I moved on after a few months to a company called McLaren's.

McLaren's was fine, but I was not there long before I heard about a job at a munitions factory called Barnbow, and that they paid good money. I went home and told my wife that I was going to try to get a job there. I always got Norma's input before I made a big decision like that. Sometimes she had advice, sometimes she just provided a friendly ear. We had two sons and I was always busy. We needed to carve out time for ourselves, if only to talk about how our day went.

The first thing to do was to find out where the factory was. I knew it was a place called Crossgates, but neither my wife nor I knew where Crossgates was. Eventually I found out where the factory was and made my way there. It was way over the other side of Leeds to where we lived, so going on the bike was out of the question. Cars were far more popular here than in Jamaica, but I didn't have a licence and didn't see the need for one. The only place I went was work anyway. Maybe it was a holdover from my childhood, when the only people who had cars were wealthy or needed it for their jobs. It was different in England, but I suppose I never got with the program.

On arrival at the gatehouse, the gatekeeper (there is a theme going on here!) looked at me and said there were no jobs available. I'd learned from last time that appealing to logic with the gatekeeper was a fool's errand, they were beyond reasoning. I simply asked to see the labour officer, but the gatekeeper knocked me back again and insisted that there were no vacancies. As I was about to leave another gatekeeper arrived and asked me why I was there.

I mentioned to him that I had been informed that there were employment opportunities there. He was not sure, so he got on the phone and told the labour officer that there was a young Jamaican lad looking for a job. I was told to go up to the office, the gateman had to show me the way to the office, and as we walked towards the office we had a chat about cricket. The man was a big cricket fan and was interested to hear about our Caribbean Cricket Club. The labour officer turned out to be an ex-RAF squadron leader. He had been in charge of some West Indian servicemen during his time in the RAF and knew that we West Indians were good workers.

The interview went well, and the man was keen to employ me, but unfortunately because Barnbow was a munitions factory (they built tanks for the British army), there was a clause in the company handbook, that said only persons born in the UK or its dominions could be employed by the company. With Jamaica being just a colony, this meant that I could not be employed there. However, the labour officer wanted to see if an exception could be made. 'You are ex-RAF after all. Leave it to me, and I will see what I can do,' he told me. All I could do then was wait, to see what would happen.

I was playing dominoes with friends Lawson, Clovis and Pennycook a few hours after the interview and I told them about the vacancies at Barnbow. The money being offered was good, the best we'd seen in our line of work, so they decided to try their luck. They all had interviews, and a few weeks later all three had managed to get employment at Barnbow. I hadn't heard anything back yet. I could not understand why. I was first there and had told them about the jobs.

Then I received a letter from my mother. Two Englishmen and a Jamaican policeman had been to the house to interview her and Papa, to gather information regarding my political views. Mama was very worried about the visit from those men and thought that I had got myself into some kind of trouble. She was most relieved when she found out that it was all to do with a job application. The men also went to see the church parson, but he was new to the area and did not know me. However, he knew my family, who all went to his church. I also found out that letters had been sent to various government offices seeking information, eventually a letter arrived, saying that I could be employed at Barnbow.

I was working on my machine at McLaren's when the foreman came to see me. 'You are wanted in the labour office,' he told me.

I finished the batch of components I was working on and went down to the office. This was the first time I'd been called into the labour office, I thought that I was going to be sacked.

I got to the office and the receptionist told me, 'You are wanted upstairs.' I didn't even know there was an upstairs. I felt like I was walking to my execution. I went slowly, wondering what would happen if I just turned back and continued working. Taking far longer than it should have, I found myself at the personnel manager's office.

He sat me down and said, 'Barnbow have been in touch, and they would like you to go work for them. You start Monday,' and that was that. I didn't even have to give notice.

I later found out that those West Indian men who had remained in the UK at the end of the war had already been vetted, and they were all a few years older than me, which I think made a difference. With Lawson being with me on the *Windrush*, how he managed to be vetted so quickly, I never found out.

As I said earlier, because I had not been an apprentice engineer, I could only get semi-skilled employment. This meant that my basic pay was not as good as that of a skilled man, so I had to do piecework to make up my wages. Piecework is when a single component is given a monetary value. The more components you produce, the more money one could make.

My first few weeks at Barnbow were a disaster. I would go to the foreman's office for a job, he would look on the job board, take out a job and give it to me. It was only for two, three or four components to do.

'How do you expect me to make any money?' I would ask.

I always got the same answer, 'that's all there is for you.' To make any real money I needed to be given jobs of sixty or more components.

Things came to a head one day, when after finishing whatever job the foreman had given me that morning I went back to him to ask for another one. He had a look at the board, which was full of jobs, turned round and just said, 'sorry nothing for you.' I simply walked away and sat on a bench near my machine with my paper, checking out the horses. Soon enough the senior foreman came.

'Gardner, why aren't you working?' he asked me.

'There's no work for me.' I said.

'There's a lot of work to be done, why haven't you been to the foreman?'

'I have. He told me there's no work for me.' The man was shocked and we went to the office. He looked at the board, picked out a job and gave it to me. This turned out to be a very lucrative job, with up to 50 components to do. My foreman was not happy about it, he'd been saving all the good jobs for his mates, but he could not say anything about it. From then on, I started to get better and more rewarding jobs.

While at Barnbow I had another run in with the union, I had a bad accident, I was lifting a component to put on the machine when I slipped and damaged my knee, which laid me off work for almost six months. I was under the impression that I could get some help with sick pay from the union. I went to the union office virtually on my hands and knees, thanks to my injury.

I explained my position to the committee, they didn't care. They offered me three half-crowns. I threw the money back at them saying that I had a family to feed. The next six months were lean. We had some money saved though. Thank God we had not moved out yet. We had to lean on our friends. I am a proud man, I would never beg or take charity, but I was able to lean on my friends in these tough times the way they had had to lean on me in their own difficult times.

I'd been working so hard. Working non-stop for years, now I found it hard to walk. Maybe I needed a break, but I felt like my purpose had been taken away. I was frustrated, the pain, the lack of mobility, the money worries just added to my despair. But light can be found in even the darkest places. I was home all the time. I got to spend time with my children. I got to put Howard and Roger to bed, to bathe them and burp them. I got to see Norma more, to have lunch and dinner with her. We had the time to wake up together and go to bed together. It wasn't an easy six months, not by a long shot, but it may have been the best six months of our marriage. Still, our savings were running low and there's only so much you can save money on. As soon as I could walk well enough I was back at work. There was still pain, but we have to bear that sometimes.

I returned to work only to be told that I had not kept up with my union subs. How could I when I could barely feed my family? This meant I was no longer a member of the union. I was not allowed to use the machines and could only do a labouring job. Alternatively, I could leave. I had to accept that because even if I found another job, there was no chance of employment as a machine operator if I was not a union member. The last thing I wanted to do was to spend my life labouring (no disrespect to labourers intended) so I decided to bide my time and see how things panned out.

I was still classed as a semi-skilled engineer, which meant that I should not really be working as a labourer. So, after three weeks of general labouring, I was called to a meeting with the labour officer and union representatives. One of the union men at the meeting was the one who had opposed us joining the union a few years before, so I was expecting a bit of an argument. Just before we walked into the meeting the labour officer pulled me to one side, and said, 'whatever happens just say "yes." Everything has been sorted, so just do not get angry.'

So, we went into the meeting room, there were three men sat there talking. They continued talking when I came in, not even acknowledging my presence. It was as if I was not there. Eventually they turned to me.

'Would you like to be back in the union?' asked the man who had almost had a fit when I joined.

'Yes,' I said, doing what I was told.

'Good,' one of the other men said. 'You can start working on the machines again on Monday morning.' I don't know what I was expecting, but not that. Apparently it was that easy. Though it made me wonder why it hadn't been done already. Not to complain though, I was back in the union, and everything was right as rain again.

Even though I had trouble with the union in the early days, I became a very strong union man. I would tell any new arrival from the West Indies to always join whatever union was affiliated to the job they were doing. It was job protection, in those days if you were new to the country job protection was as good as gold, and twice as rare.

If I borrowed from anyone when I was down, I made sure to pay them back as soon as I was up. Otherwise it was back to saving for a house and working like a dog. I exchanged the difficulties of not working for the difficulties of being away from home. I missed Norma and the kids terribly now. Every morning with a heavy heart and a bad knee I would wake up to leave my family. Every night I spent at work was a night with my family I had to miss, time I'd never get back.

In spring 1954, I found out that another child was on the way. We'd already been desperate to move into our own home, but now we had to move. I'd heard about a firm of solicitors who were buying houses and doing them up, mainly to rent to West Indians, that firm was Walker, Charlesworth and Forster. I went to see Mr Charlesworth, at first to talk about renting a property, but we ended up talking about Norma and I buying a house.

When I mentioned to my colleagues that I was thinking of buying my own house they were shocked. In those days the ordinary working man lived mainly in council houses. Even Norma's own family were surprised when they found out she was going to buy a house. Yet I was not the only one buying a house around that time, most of the cricket team like Charlie Dawkins, Errol James and Glen English were also investing in property.

The only criteria I asked for was that the house had to be near a school. Mr Charlesworth had the perfect property, not too far from the house on Regent Terrace, with an infant and junior school at the end of the road and a secondary school a ten-minute walk away. A deal was done, and the house was purchased by Mr Charlesworth, and I paid him, which made it easier for Norma and I because we didn't have to go and try to get a mortgage at a bank or building society.

We moved into 23 Brudenell Mount towards the end of 1954. Soon after, in December 1954, Laraine Gardner, my first daughter, was born.

Chapter Sixteen

23 Brudenell Mount had originally been bought by the firm of solicitors to rent out to two families. A couple of the houses in the street already had two families living in them. In the cellar a large cooking range and toilet had been installed (not in the same room). There was a kitchen and a living room on the ground floor. We didn't have a carpet in the kitchen, but we did have lino on the floor.

In the living room, behind the settee was a large mahogany table which we all sat around at mealtimes. As the family grew, I had to keep buying dining room chairs, so in the end I had various styles of dining chairs around the table. This table was not just a dining table, it had multiple uses. It became a desk for the children to do their homework, it was used as an ironing board, also as a games table, the kids playing their board games on it and it was even used as a table tennis table, the table was thick enough to attach a net on to it. I also had an old-fashioned wind-up gramophone player in the living room that only played 78 rpm records. Norma and I would dance to those records sometimes. We never got to go out dancing anymore.

There were two bedrooms and a bathroom on the first floor and then two attic rooms, which were later converted into bedrooms as the children grew up. So this house had two toilets, which was very unusual, many houses at this time had outside toilets, where you had to walk down the street to use it. There was no central heating in those days. The only heating in the house was a small hearth. In winter we would all huddle around the fire to try and keep warm.

Mr Charlesworth suggested to me that to help with the repayments we should let out the cellar. I was keen to get some more money in, but Norma was not really interested in adding more people to our household. Eventually we reached a point where we needed more money and we rented the cellar out to a woman with a young child.

Now with a mortgage and the beginning of a large family, I was working seven days a week, including doing overtime three nights a week. When I was home, I was usually tired. Norma was tired too, I don't think anyone's ever said raising three children is easy. This meant that my wife and I did not have much of a social life. Norma's relationship with her parents was better now, but I still wanted nothing to do with her father. He seemed to soften towards me when he realised he was missing out on watching his grandchildren grow up, but our relationship could never heal after our first meeting. Norma's mother and father probably always would have found it difficult to accept me anyway. I had got their daughter pregnant at a young age.

This is all to say that getting a babysitter was difficult. I had a complicated relationship with her parents and mine were too far away, unfortunately they had never even met my kids. I'd have loved to fly to Jamaica, see the family and show Norma and the children the place where I was born and raised. It was never on the cards though, we were scraping by.

My wife did patch up her relationship with her parents. Not because we needed a babysitter, but because she missed them. Because of that first meeting with my father-in-law, I would not have anything to do with him. After we got settled in the house, Norma's parents started to visit. Eventually it would be happening every Tuesday. I would be getting ready to go to work or go to the gym. I would pop my head into the living room.

My father-in-law would look up and say, 'how are you?' or 'hello.'

I would just reply, 'I'm well thank you,' then walk out of the room. I could not bring myself to try and be friendly with him. I refused to give him the chance to get to know me, but he adored the kids and doted on them. I would have nothing to do with him, but I was glad the kids could have that relationship with their grandparents. Norma had an older sister, Madge, and two younger siblings, Peter and Irene, so the children had aunties and an uncle nearby at least. I had a good relationship with Norma's brother Peter. Irene, Peter and his wife, Helga, were constant visitors to our house.

It was good to have a house by the time Laraine was born. Norma and I were both delighted when our first daughter came along, but more than that we felt secure in our new home. This was the life we wanted. The Hyde Park area was known as a rough part of Leeds at the time, but it was a good house and exactly what we needed. Honestly, I never found it to be rough. I didn't have much trouble there; problems are something I can't afford.

If anything was ever said by anyone, an off-colour joke or remark about the colour of my skin, or our interracial marriage, Norma or I would nip things in the bud before anything got out of hand. Norma may have been small, but she was a strong woman and fiercely protective of her children. We would never let the children hear of any problems; we did this to protect our children from any ugliness. I have heard stories of black or mixed-race families being forced from their homes due to racism, fortunately that never happened to my family and me.

The neighbours on both sides were nice. There was Mr & Mrs Hall on one side, and the Hoy family on the other. The woman who lived in the house opposite was okay with our family, not too sure about her husband, somehow I never spoke to him. I know that there were a few people in the street who were not happy with us moving into the street. We would wave at one woman but she refused to acknowledge us. The only time she opened her mouth was to shout at the kids if a ball went into her garden.

Racism was always there, but I think it was less blatant then than it is now. Walking down the street, or on buses you would get strange looks, you may hear the odd person make a comment under their breath, but they'd never say it loudly. They wouldn't even repeat it if you asked them what they said. At job interviews, the way they asked, and the manner of the way people asked questions made you uneasy, especially in those early years.

One of the questions that really got under my skin was the way they would say, 'and where do YOU come from?' It was said in such a degrading manner. When you have a landlady of a boarding house smiling politely as she tells you that there are no rooms available, when you know for a fact there are vacant rooms in the house. There was nouse in making a fuss or arguing with people, just move on and hope that the next interview is successful, and the next landlady will be more accommodating. I wouldn't want to work with a racist anyway.

I was one of those people who had a sixth sense about people and if I went into a pub, I could tell by looking at someone, that by the way they looked at me that they were trouble, so I would stand as far away from them as I could.

When I have watched documentaries regarding racism on TV, it seems to me that the later arrivals from commonwealth countries of colour appeared to have had more trouble than us early pioneers. It may not be worse for them, it is just the impression I get.

Racism aside, we were thriving and happy. I had the life I wanted. Norma and I were still finding time for each other when we could and continuing to expand our family. Edmund Gardner was born in August 1956, Maxine Gardner in December 1957.

With most of the West Indians now starting families, cricket became more of a family affair. In those early days, the team would meet at Clarendon Place and later Regent Terrace if it was an away game and we would all get on to a coach to take us to the ground. Then, as we all started to buy our own properties in the various parts of Leeds, Chapeltown became our meeting place for our away games. This was the area of Leeds where the majority of the West Indians who came in the late fifties and early sixties settled. The team would practise on Tuesday and Thursday nights. Due to work and family I couldn't always make it, but I'd go along whenever possible. We played league matches on a Saturday and would have a friendly or a cup match on the Sunday. I'd even occasionally play for the Barnbow team, time allowing.

When not playing cricket, working or spending time with my family, I was gambling. Gambling has always been a passion of mine. Am I addicted? Probably so, but I never let it control me. I don't believe my family ever suffered because I liked a bet (they might disagree). I never played poker anymore, due to players cheating, but I still enjoyed betting on the horses. So Saturday became my horse racing day.

I acquired a TV during the mid-fifties. I would arrive home from work at lunchtime on Saturday and study the form of the horses in the paper. I would run to the bookies on the next street up from ours, place my bet, and run back to the house to watch the race on TV. In the summer when the kids were playing in the street, they would often follow me as I was running up to the bookie. More often than not, when the winner had passed the winning post, the horse that I had backed would still be running while I was on the way back up to the bookie to place my next bet.

Thursday night was the time to do the football pools, the working man's way to becoming a millionaire. Littlewoods and Vernon's pools were the two companies who provided the biggest pay-outs. Every now and again I would ask one of the children to fill out a pool coupon, hoping that because they did not know what they were actually doing I might get lucky. Unsurprisingly, it never worked, but it was about more than just winning. I chased that feeling of anticipation; watching a horse race, checking the football scores on a Saturday afternoon, it took me back to that first buzz I got watching the men play dominoes, all those years back.

Chapter Seventeen

There was bliss in the Gardner household in 1959. We were expecting our sixth child and it all seemed to be running like clockwork. My job was going well and I was making good money, even with all of our children, we were doing well. Norma was great at budgeting, and we saved on clothes as the children were wearing their older siblings hand-me-downs or something Norma had knitted for them herself. She also made miracles in the kitchen. Norma was a wonderful cook.

However, no summer is endless. Norma's father died in March 1959. Before his death he and Norma's mother would come over every Tuesday, they'd take Howard and Roger almost every weekend and even took Howard on a few holidays. I never got my head around how he doted on the children so much, but I didn't need to understand it.

Our relationship remained tense, we'd settled into our own uneasy ritual of half-greeting each other when I'd pass him as I left the house. There was no love lost between us, but I did attend his funeral, out of respect for Norma and her family. Unfortunately, due to work I was late getting there. Afterwards, Norma and her family all went for a drink, but I didn't go with them as it didn't feel right.

In May 1959 we had our sixth child, Sharon. Not one month after she was born, I was made redundant at Barnbow, after six and a half years. I'd been making good money at Barnbow and almost immediately after losing my job, I found work at English Electric, an engineering company in Bradford. The pay was poor there, it was just a stopgap until I found something better. Three weeks into the job, a friend told me about work at another factory in Bradford, an American owned company called International Harvesters. In Britain, they built tractors, but in the USA, they built big yellow school buses, buses for the Forces and articulated lorry cabs.

On arriving at the factory, the man at the gate gave me the usual answer, no vacancies here. I don't think I even argued with him, just turned around and started walking away. However, someone who I had worked with at McLaren's factory recognised me and shouted for the gateman to stop me from leaving the premises. I had a job interview and just like that, I had a new job.

The interviews themselves were nearly all the same:

'What type of training do you have?'

'What experience do you have?'

'What did you do in the RAF?'

'What's Jamaica like, do you miss it?'

'Do you enjoy living in England?'

I don't know if those last two questions were out of genuine interest or to see if I was a flight-risk, but I always said yes. I'd made a beautiful home here.

At Harvesters my job title was radial driller, I drilled and taped holes in a component. The component was a cylinder head for tractors, drills and taps were always snapping in the hole (taps are what were used to put a screw thread in a drilled hole). The company employed a man just to remove the broken bits, but he was slow. I had found a way to remove these broken pieces fairly quickly so I asked the foreman if I could have a go at removing the said broken bits. He said that I could and was impressed by my method. He asked me if I would spend the weekend just working on the damaged cylinder heads. This upset a few of my workmates, as I was getting overtime when some were being made redundant. They even confronted me about it, but I told them to stop moaning. I was prepared to do a job that many did not want to do or were unable to do.

As I mentioned before, for most of my working life I did piece work, as this was the best way for a semi-skilled man to improve his wages; the more components we produced the more money we could make. All engineering companies had setters, who would come and set the machines up with the correct tooling. I was never happy with that arrangement, a skilled foreman would come to set up whatever machine I was working on, which would restrict the amount of money that I could make as it took so long to set the machine up.

So, I would set about changing the set-up of the jobs to suit my way of working, just by using different tooling and drills and speeding up the machine. Some of the working practices in these factories had been that way for decades, and the setters, chargehands and foremen were not happy with me changing the old ways. I didn't care. I won most of them over when I showed them that the finished product was just as good if not better with my faster way of working. There were still a few who didn't like it, but that was their own problem.

This happened at just about every factory that I worked at, there were always easier and faster ways to produce components. I was not maximising efficiency and output for the company, I was doing it for myself to make money. At every factory I worked at, I worked hard, but I also worked smart.

In May 1960, Diane Gardner was born. Soon after I moved on to work permanent nights. It wasn't easy, but it was my choice. The work was there, and I could do it. I was responsible for my family, and so whenever the opportunity to make more money came along, I took it. In late 1961, Norma gave birth to a boy. Unfortunately he died at birth, before we had even given him a name. That was a hard time for Norma and me, but it ultimately brought us closer.

I want to clarify that my life with Norma was not just filled with work, babymaking and childrearing. It was a special relationship, we very rarely fought or disagreed. We didn't get to go out much and our dance-hall days were behind us, but we still had our fun, such as when Jamaica gained independence from the UK, in 1962. I put the new Jamaican flag up in the house. The children had no idea what was going on, but they joined in the celebrations anyway. I remember being invited to an Independence party in Manchester. It was a brilliant party, even the Jamaican High Commissioner was there. Wray and Nephew rum was going down nicely, you could hear the popping of the champagne corks. Some bright spark thought it might be a good idea to mix the rum and the champagne, which turned out not to be a good idea for me. It was a good job that I was near a door, I just made it onto the street before I vomited all over the road. A number of people were sick that night.

That year we also went to a dance with my colleagues at International Harvesters. It was the first time Norma had met any of my co-workers, not including my friends, of course. I walked into the dance hall and people asked where she was. She had just popped into the ladies' room, when she walked into the room my workmates were taken aback by how stunning she was. The next day at work everyone kept asking me how I ended up with someone so lovely, and I was getting comments about having a movie star wife.

We also had fun with the kids when we could. During the summertime International Harvesters would have family open days. So along with other workers from the factory I was able to take my children to the factory where they would have a tour of the factory and were able to ride on the tractors. Harvesters also had their own showground, which was in Greengates, a couple of miles from the factory, where they set up swings and roundabouts for the children, organised races, horse riding, sporting events and other types of amusement.

We rarely got the opportunity to go on holiday. In fact, I never went on holiday with my kids. I left the entertainment side of things to Norma; she would take the children on daytrips to Blackpool when we could afford it. Gladstone and I did take Howard and Roger to Filey on a day trip in 1956. We went to the camp where we did our RAF training, but it had been converted back to a holiday camp, so we were not allowed to show them around it. The only other place I took Howard and Roger was to Elland Road one night to watch Leeds United. This was at the beginning of the Don Revie era, and they were in the old division two league. If I remember correctly, it was a game between Leeds and Plymouth and ended up as a 1-1 draw. Both boys became big Leeds United fans that night. However, my favourite sport will always be cricket and I tried t pass down that love to my children.

We had some very good players, a couple could possibly have played test cricket if they had stayed in the West Indies. For home games the wives who attended would do the sandwiches. Norma never went, we had too many young children to look after, and she hated cricket. I would often take Howard with me, and as the other children grew up would take them along to the game, and the children of the other players who went would all play together.

As I said Norma hated cricket, but without her the team could have folded soon after being set up. The team, in their wisdom, made me treasurer. I was supposed to collect 10 shillings (the equivalent of £15 today) a week from the players, in order to buy the equipment, but that was easier said than done. Every week players would have an excuse not to pay me anything. It wasn't until Errol James became our president that things picked up moneywise.

One week we needed some new bats, but we didn't have enough money in the kitty to buy any. We were going to have to cancel the upcoming match and possibly disband the team due to the lack of funds and equipment. I went home and told Norma, she told me to go buy some bats out of my wages.

'We have enough money for food,' she told me, 'and you and the team need equipment.' The thought hadn't even occurred to me, and Norma knew that I wouldn't have unless she suggested it. Norma was very good like that, without her telling me to buy things the team may not be playing today. We even had a bat that had been signed by the touring West Indian team at the time. It might be worth a fortune by now if we'd preserved it, but we had to use it one day because we had broken our only bats during a match.

Whenever the West Indian test cricket team played a test match at Headingley, it was always a time of great excitement. The Caribbean Cricket team would hold a reception for them at a club called the Lamport, which was on Chapletown Road in Leeds. I would go along to meet the team and a good time was had by all. Meeting players the stature of Sir Garfield Sobers, Wes Hall and Lance Gibbs was always a pleasure.

I also played in a few cricket games for International Harvesters. I would not take my cricket gear to work, I would get Howard and Roger to bring it for me. Howard was ten, Roger was eight. The ground where we played was in Greengates, Bradford, a 45-minute bus journey from our home. My teammates would tell me off for making two young boys get on the bus by themselves and bring my equipment all the way from Leeds, but I never saw anything wrong with it. I don't think they minded bringing it, if they did, they never mentioned it. They were excited to help their dad and at that age it almost seemed like an adventure to them.

Howard and Roger being the oldest children, they were often left in charge of the younger ones. Diane was very sick and in and out of hospital a lot. When Norma went to see our baby in hospital or had to go out shopping while I was at work, Howard and Roger took care of the younger children. Social services would probably have something to say about it nowadays. I think I just had a different approach to raising kids, due to my upbringing in Jamaica. My co-workers were mainly white and English, they had a way of raising kids and I had a way of raising mine. Interestingly, I never felt a cultural barrier between me and Norma. There was never really any friction between us; since we had met everything always seemed to feel so natural between us. We agreed on almost all matters when it came to the children, particularly our desire for more.

In October 1963, Paula Gardner was born. Norma went into labour early with Paula. I sent Howard out to phone for the ambulance. the public phone box was in the next street, but before he had got back to the house, I had already delivered Paula. The ambulance arrived about 20 minutes later to take both mother and daughter to hospital.

I was proud of how Howard handled that situation; he had just turned twelve but was so cool in a crisis when his mother needed him. I am proud of all my children. As parents we always try to fix the mistakes our parents made with us, but we're destined to fail and make our own mistakes. My father was a firm disciplinarian. I didn't want to be as strict as him, but he was an admirable man and a very good father. I learned a lot from him. It's hard to not be strict when your idea of parenting is discipline. I was quite strict as a father. At mealtimes everyone had to sit at the table, even when one of them had finished eating they were not allowed to leave the table, unless they asked for permission. I believed in physical discipline, and would occasionally spank the boys if they got out of line, but never with the same frequency, intensity or pleasure which my father had when he doled out these punishments. Education and manners were the main things I instilled in them, and I'm pleased to say that wherever Norma or I took my children people would always comment on their manners.

When I was at home, like most men who had been working all day, I would often doze off while watching TV. I would put a newspaper over my head to block out the light and the children would get up to turn the TV over. As soon as they touched the knob on the TV, my voice would boom from below the paper, 'leave the TV alone. I'm watching that.' Whichever child had got up to turn the TV over would sit down. I could then relax and go back to my gentle sleep.

As I write this and strain to remember the time I have spent with my family, I realise that I did not do much with the children. I was busy, but when I was not working I could have done more with the children. Less cricket and gambling, again, I wonder if I inherited this trait from my father. I saw my role mainly as a provider. To provide is, of course, important, but there are a million important facets to being a father. I'm afraid I neglected some while my children were growing up.

I did always ensure that my children had a great Christmas. It was a herculean effort on my part trying to buy presents for so many children. The build up towards Christmas would start in November when Norma would begin making Christmas cakes. The children would have to creep around the house, any vibration and the cake could collapse in the middle. The week before Christmas Day would see Norma and I taking it in turns to go to the Leeds market to get the food, dragging either Howard or Roger to help with the bags. The turkey was ordered a few weeks before the day, we always ordered a big one, around 20 lbs/9kg that would just about fit in our oven.

The day itself was a special chaotic bliss, with Norma trying to do the dinner, some children playing with their toys, some reading books, or some trying to watch the TV.

Chapter Eighteen

The swinging sixties were well underway. I was working seven days a week. Bingo halls were starting to be set up, many of them taking over old cinemas. Bingo became my new obsession. Horse racing was slowly relegated to second place, but still a passion of mine. Some Saturdays I'd come from work, bet on the horses, eat with my family then go straight to bingo. However, there were bigger changes happening than the rise of bingo, you could sense that things were beginning to change.

The music seemed different, fresher, livelier. Fashion appeared more colourful; the world was starting to move away from the drab grey post-war years. The USA had a young new president John F. Kennedy, who spoke of equality for African Americans. In the UK, laws on censorship, abortion and homosexuality were being relaxed. The Race Relations Act came into force in 1965; this was supposed to help stop racial discrimination. Did it help? I suppose up to a point it did. More places, like some clubs and pubs, were opened up to people of colour and a black person could not be turned down a job due to their colour. I didn't feel an immediate tangible difference, but of course you can't legislate racism away, and changing attitudes takes time.

As the children got older, it was harder to shield them from ugly realities. I suppose a parent's job cannot be to shield his child from the world's ugliness, but prepare them to face its harshness. All the children had white friends who lived in the street or nearby. For a few years we were the only mixed-race family in the street, then the Okonofua family moved in at the far end of the street. The husband, Felix, was of African descent, his wife, Betty, was white and born in England. Their kids quickly became friends with ours and we were at each other's houses quite often.

When Roger was twelve, he had an argument with a girl in the street. I believe it escalated and it became physical, leading to Roger pushing the girl. The girl told her father, who came out of the house and grabbed Roger. Roger's friend David Taylor ran to our house to get me. I ran out of the house, the man had Roger by the scruff of the neck up against a wall.

'Get your hands off my boy!' I shouted, running over to them. 'Get off of him!' I must have said it about four times before the man let go and turned around. He was a big man, about 6'4. He was about to say something when I hit him with a couple of body shots, still shouting, 'get your hands off my boy.' The man swung a punch at me, but I ducked and I kept hitting him to the body. He went down.

Crumpled on the floor, he covered up and asked me to stop. I obliged. I've never hit a man when he's down. Plus, seeing the man fold had made my anger subside. When I saw him manhandling my son, I couldn't control myself. I can barely remember the aftermath, some more angry words were said and he told me to keep my son away from his daughter, I had no problem with that and we went our separate ways. A few days later, I received a letter from the man's solicitor saying any more incidents like that and they would take the matter further. In hindsight it should have been me going to the police and having him arrested for assaulting Roger. It's funny, despite some positive experiences with the police I'd grown quite distrustful of the long arm of the law.

Around this time, Howard was having some problems with a group of lads when he was in secondary school. The leader of the boys hated anyone who was not white. This boy even managed to turn some of Howard's close friends, who he had known since infant and junior school, into racists. These were boys whose houses he would go to to play with them, boys who would come to our house and play and have dinner. They started to call him racist names. He didn't care about the ringleader, but losing his friends really hurt him. Howard has only told me this recently, unfortunately I did not know this was happening at the time.

Around this time a few families who had arrived post-*Windrush* from the Caribbean were on the move again, this time to Canada. Norma and I discussed emigrating to Canada and we made enquiries. After having spoken to the Canadian office, we were told that our family was too large and that there were no apartments available which could accommodate us. Norma and I weren't too disappointed. We'd been interested in a change of scenery, but we were quite happy where we were. Starting over in Canada was interesting, but all our friends were here. Her family was here and I still had Gladstone nearby.

My relationship with Gladstone was never better. He came to stay in our crowded house for a while. I can't even tell you how we managed to find the space, but we did. He stayed for some months while he found a job and a house. He could never have worn out his welcome though. I loved having him there, so did Norma, it was another person to watch the kids. They all loved their uncle. Though he stayed with us for four months, it felt like he was gone in a flash. This time he didn't leave because he was fed up with me but because he needed to move on with his life. He was looking to put down roots in Leeds before he married his long-time girlfriend, Ruth.

Due to working most weekends, I could not play cricket as much as I would like to, so I decided to leave the team, but I would still go along to watch and would play in the occasional friendly. The last time I played was at Kirkheaton Cricket Club, which would have been in 1966. It was the only time my son Howard and I played in a competitive match together.

I stopped participating in any type of sport in the mid-sixties. Cricket was all I had time for anyway, I loved all sports, but cricket will always be number one in my heart, I was more of an observer of the other sports. I did do a spot of bodybuilding in the fifties, before I packed it all in. I used to go to a gym run by a professional bodybuilder named Reg Park in Leeds to train. I always wanted to be a big man, I don't mean tall but muscular, but watching Reg Park and his friend made me realise how much of a task it was. Bodybuilding was a lifestyle, his work ethic was impressive, but the weights he was lifting astounded me. I could have dedicated my life to bodybuilding and never been able to compete with these men.

One night after doing a heavy training session, instead of having a cooling off and wind down session, I went straight to work. Halfway through the night my body felt like jelly and I was so tired that I thought that I was going to collapse. That was one of my last training sessions; Reg emigrated to South Africa soon afterwards. He went on to make a couple of films and also won the Mr Universe and Mr Great Britain competitions a couple of times. It is said he inspired Arnie Schwarzenegger to become a bodybuilder.

The only sport I kept up with was running, mainly for the bus. Being a typical Jamaican I was always leaving the house at the last minute, knowing that I had only seconds to get to the bus stop. Despite no longer playing, I still enjoyed watching sport. I even had two TVs on the go at Brundenell Mount at that time. One on top of the other. I would watch a sport on one TV, usually cricket, and have the horse racing on the other. I also love music and before the days of Walkmans and MP3 players I had a little transistor radio, which had one earpiece. Quite often I would be seen jigging when stood at the bus stop or walking down the street.

I had my pleasures and my vices and my beautiful family. My life was not perfect, but I have no regrets. It was a great life, but of course as in any life, there was always work to do. I worked at Harvesters throughout the 60s. I trained as a first aider there. Time was set aside during shifts for the other trainees and I to our first aid training. This was to be my last full-time job, after many years on the shop floor working as a machinist.

One night a member of the management came to see me. The nurse who worked on the night shift was retiring, for some reason he wanted me to take over her role. I jumped at the chance to move into being a full time first aider. I'd wanted to be a doctor when I was younger and this was the closest I'd get to my former dream. Because of my refusal to learn British history, all avenues of further education were closed off to me. This job at first did make me wonder what could have been, but that soon went out of my head. What is the point of wondering what could have been?

· Later, I asked the nurse what to expect from the job and she told me that I would be pleasantly surprised. On the first Monday in my new role, I turned up at work in a shirt and tie. My foreman asked me what I was doing dressed like that. I turned around and proudly told him that I was now in charge of the first aid room. He asked me when this happened and I realised I had forgot to tell him that I would no longer be working for him.

I enjoyed my time as a first aider, it was the best job I ever had. Whenever I left a job of my own volition it was because of pay, that was what mattered to me. So, I had a big shock when I got my first paycheque as the first-aider on the night shift, I was earning more than I did working a big dirty/greasy machine. Most nights when I got to work, I would put my feet up on the desk, turn on the radio and read a book until I was called upon. There were many nights when I wasn't needed at all. I was in my early forties then. After working so hard for so long, on my feet all day, it was nice to put my feet up at work. I felt like I'd really made it.

The job itself was mainly dealing with cuts or removing splinters. If there was any serious incident, I had to call for an ambulance, but I would deal with the patient until help arrived. The worst incident I had was when a call came into the medical room to say a man had collapsed. I called for an ambulance before I went to look at the man, but as soon as I got to him, I could see that it was too late, he had already passed away.

It was a big factory, and I didn't know the man, but I learnt later that the man made his own booze. People speculated that's what led to his untimely death. I never found out the cause of death, but it was the worst thing to happen on my shift.

Chapter Nineteen

Unfortunately, all good things come to an end. The world seems to change every day, change seemed to occur much faster in England than it did in Jamaica. The years rolled on from the late sixties to the early seventies. My oldest children, Howard, Roger and Sharon, got married. My youngest, Paula, was getting into her teens. Perhaps not always forward, but everything and everyone was moving and I stayed the same, set in my ways. There were times I drank a lot, but I'd never say I was an alcoholic. There were times all I seemed to do was work, but I felt it was necessary. There were times where I spent all my free time gambling, maybe I was addicted. I was never destitute because of gambling, but maybe I enjoy it too much.

This is all to say that I have my vices and my flaws. One thing I don't think you can ever do is spend too much time with your family, spend too many nights at home, tuck your children into bed too often. Unfortunately I could never be accused of that. I've lived a long life, but it all goes in the blink of an eye. Sometimes I still wonder how life breezed past so quickly, just yesterday I was excitedly boarding the HMT *Empire Windrush*.

This isn't to say that I have regrets, I don't live life with regrets. I believe I have lived my life to the fullest and I wouldn't change a thing. When I say I made a mistake, the action is not to regret it, but to never repeat it. In the '70s, when I wasn't working nights, I'd be at the bingo on weekdays. On the weekend I'd be out for a drink. 23 Brudenell Mount was chaos in the sixties, always teeming with life. I had eight children, they would bring their friends around constantly, to play, to hang out, to have dinner. There was never a moment's peace in my house. It's exactly how we wanted it.

The seventies were much quieter, most of my children were out of the house. In the mid-seventies, when my youngest daughter Paula was in her teens and we had more time to focus on each other, I should have been asking Norma to go out more. To get a drink with me, to go dancing again, get a bite to eat, anything she wanted. We were both going out more at that time, just not together. We were only in our late forties at this time, no spring chickens, but so much life left. Yet I never got around to it.

Both of my parents died during the seventies. I didn't have the money to go back to Jamaica for my mother's funeral, most of the kids were gone by then and every day I could feel Norma and I drifting apart. It's harder when it happens like that, when you lose each other by millimetres. It's imperceptible, you don't notice it, you can't talk about it, or fix it, but eventually it reveals itself and breaks everything down like rot. I felt so alone. My father died not too long after my mother and I couldn't miss another parent's funeral. With the help of a bank loan I was able to attend my father's funeral. That was the first time I had been home since my arrival in England on the *Windrush*. It was good to see everyone and to be back, but it was only for a short while. Underneath my happiness to see my family was the grief I felt at losing my parents I'd barely spoken to them in decades and now I never could again. My parents never managed to visit me in the UK and they never got to meet their grandchildren.

In hindsight, I'm sure this impacted me more than I realised. How could I not be affected by losing both of my parents within a year of each other? I didn't really talk about my grief though, not even to Norma. I wish I'd had something to consume me, but I couldn't throw myself into work like I could as a young man. Now I was at a desk with my feet up, turning the radio up in an attempt to block the sound of my thoughts.

At this time I was seeing the regulars at bingo more than I was seeing my own family. Jean was a friend of Norma and me, she had recently lost her husband, Spooner. We'd been there for her and she was usually at bingo when I went, we'd sit together and joke around. A few days before Christmas it all came to a head. A Christmas card came to the house addressed to Mr and Mrs Gardner. Norma opened it. The card read 'Merry Christmas to Jean and Ford', someone from bingo had assumed Jean and I were a couple. Norma accused me of things, none of which were true. To me, my relationship with Jean was all above board. I had my lines and boundaries that I would never cross, but in hindsight I see what was happening. How close Jean and I were getting, while Norma and I were growing further apart. In those years we became more like housemates than husband and wife.

Around this time, Diane left the house too. She had been offered a job to work in a hotel in Jersey. When she arrived at the hotel the manager took one look at her and said, 'we don't employ your kind on this island.' I suppose she should have put 'Black' on her CV or words to that effect. Not knowing what to do she walked out of the hotel and sat on a bench where she just broke down and started to cry.

Some people seeing her in distress gathered round her to find what was wrong. She told them what had happened, and some of the locals told her that the people on the island were not like the manager of that hotel. A manager of another hotel was in the group of people who had gathered around her offering to help and he offered her a job on the spot. Diane accepted and she ended up working on the island for a few years, as far as I know she didn't encounter an incident like that again in Jersey.

With Diane gone, it was just Norma and I in the house. After a lifetime together, after eight kids, we were like strangers, we didn't know how to be alone together. I remember when we were younger and every moment seemed to be spent trying to steal seconds alone with each other.

I could tell you every detail of my romance with Norma, but no one can ever understand a marriage like the two people in it and we didn't understand it at all.

The worst thing is I didn't even see the signs. We weren't even communicating in a friendly manner together, we were almost avoiding each other, yet I was surprised when I came home from work one day and the house was empty. That was in June 1983, we had been together for 33 years, known each other almost 40 years. In all those years we never had a holiday, not even a weekend away. We should have spent more time together, if we had maybe that time when there was just the two of us things may have been different. Maybe not.

As I said, everything was changing. Fighting the current isn't sustainable, so I've always tried to go alone with it. A year before Norma left, I was made redundant due to the factory closing down. Jobs in engineering were hard to come by; in the 1980s more than 90% of engineering companies closed down in the Yorkshire area. I couldn't find any more work, there was less that I was able to do at such an advanced age. I was strong and athletic in my youth, not strong like Reg Park, but strong. I felt like I could do anything in my twenties. I was now 55 years old, the men getting the jobs I was applying for were 20 or 30 years younger than me. So I decided to take early retirement, even though it would be another ten years until I could claim my Old Age Pension. I did a couple of part time jobs, working on building sites until the time came for me to receive my state pension.

Chapter Twenty

After the divorce, on Norma's insistence, we sold the house. I had wanted to convert the house and use it for student accommodation, living not far from Leeds University there was always the need for more accommodation for students, but my now ex-wife was against that idea. So, I left Brudenell Mount and I moved in with Jean to enter a new phase of my life as I neared 60.

I had known Jean for many years, ever since those early days in the Mecca. She knew Norma but did not initially hang around with her. However, the two women became close when Jean and her husband Spooner moved into the next street. When the Spooners moved to a new home in Bramley, Norma would often go visit Jean and spent a lot of time with her after her husband had passed away. As you can imagine, Norma wasn't happy and I believe she destroyed our wedding photos. I understand why she did that, but I do wish I could have included them in this book. Though it wasn't a fancy wedding, it was one of the happiest days of my life. She'd never looked more beautiful.

Jean loved to travel. Despite originally being from Jamaica, I had not really done much travelling. Jean took me to Tenerife, where she had an apartment. Over the next few years we went to Cuba, the Dominican Republic, Trinidad and Tobago and Egypt where we had a trip down the

Nile. We were in Goa when the tsunami hit India. I was quite upset when none of my family got in touch to find out if I was OK. I found out later that nobody knew I was there until I had returned home from Goa.

While we were in Cuba, Jean told me a story about her father, he was a policeman. One especially cold winter night in 1947, he had come home from duty, and told Jean about the young West Indian man that he had found shivering near to Leeds market. I couldn't believe it. She was very surprised too when I told her it was me he had been talking about.

Though semi-retired and travelling often, I was not living a simple life of luxury. Well, not always. For a short time I did a computer course at the Swarthmore Education Centre in Leeds. They run educational courses for unemployed people and for those who find it difficult to study in the more formal educational institutions. I was used to working on large industrial machines, so working on a keyboard and all the terminology involved with computers was alien to me. I still have no idea what Word or Excel is, I shudder when people mention PowerPoint. Even now I have trouble using a mobile phone, all I know is the green button to answer the phone and the red button to end the call, that's if I hear the thing.

Around this time in the mid-eighties, one of my friends who had been in London had heard a rumour that the government was in the process of finding a way to send some people back to their own countries, including West Indians. I was told that my children were safe, but that I could be sent back. At first, I did not believe him and said that he must have heard wrong. My friend was going back to London and said that he would check what was going on.

When he came back, he told me that the rumours were true and gave me some papers to fill in. I filled the form in, sent it back and I became a British citizen. It cost me £80, a decent amount of money for the time, especially as I was semi-retired. I would like my money back, but I don't think I will ever get it. It may have taken a while but in 2018, on the 70th anniversary of the *Windrush* arriving in the UK, the Windrush scandal hit the media.

During the '80s and '90s, I did not get to see very much of my children, only at birthdays and weddings. Not because Norma and I had split up and the children had taken sides, more because they were all starting their own families and as I said before, I was away a lot of the time, with Jean, on our travels.

Chapter Twenty-One

My story would not be complete without talking about my children. I feel blessed that the family is still together, and that they still all get on well with each other.

Over the years we have had some good parties. We had two parties for my ninetieth birthday, the first one was a meal with just family at the Turtle Bay, a West Indian restaurant in Leeds, and the second at my local pub The Rock, for friends and family. The landlord still talks about that night, the profit he made that night paid for his holiday that year. My niece Kay and her family came up from Hitchin, along with nephews and nieces from my ex-wife Norma's side of the family, and we were drinking and dancing all through the night. We have also had some beautiful weddings; my grandchildren really know how to put on a show.

I will give a brief history of each of my children starting with Howard. Howard did all right at school. He left school aged fifteen and started an engineering apprenticeship, which lasted five years and he qualified as a skilled engineer. Ironically, if Howard had come to work at any factory I was working at, he would earn more money than me just for being a skilled engineer. With the demise of engineering factories in the 1980s, he had to retrain and he trained to become an office equipment engineer, repairing and servicing photocopiers and printers, which he did until he retired.

Like me, Howard loves sport and music, he played rugby, football, and cricket in his teens, and by his own admission was really only making up the numbers in the teams he played for. He later took up playing squash (which is a racket ball sport), and now in his retirement years plays golf. Howard married his wife Helen in 1976 and they adopted two children Thomas and Hannah. In 1994, Howard caught pneumonia. I was not aware at the time, as I was on holiday, but it was touch and go for a while. Howard has helped me immensely with this book and I can't thank him enough.

Roger also did well at school, in fact they all did well, so I will not mention that fact again. At school he was particularly good at rugby and was a star player for the school team. As he moved into his teens, he stopped playing sports altogether. He started working for a music company when he left school, before moving onto retail management, he also worked as a DJ at various venues in the Leeds area.

Roger perhaps reminded me of myself the most out of all my children. He was married three times, to Marilyn, Marilyn (not the same woman) and Jayne, and had three children Marc, Dino, and Francesca.

He later moved to a company that provided doctors for night-time emergency cover, but due to a company takeover was unfortunately let go. He was hoping to set up his own business and had taken a part time job with the Post Office to tide him over. While working at the Post Office he had a fatal heart attack. He was 52 years old. That hit the family hard. There is not a day that passes that I don't think about my boy. The pain of losing a child is indescribable.

Next there is Laraine, she was a good sprinter at school, and I had high hopes of her being an Olympian. However, as she got older, she was not interested in going down the sporting road and I didn't push her. After leaving school she had various jobs but never made a career of any of them. She worked in retail, did office work, had a job in tailoring and worked as a barmaid for a while, before finishing her working life as a school dinner lady. She never married, but her long-term partner is Joe.

Laraine provided me with my first grandchild, who then provided me with my first great grandchild, who then went on to provide me with my first great, great grandchild. There are not many people alive with great-great-grandchildren. She has three children, Samantha, Mark, and Ryan.

Now onto my third son Edmund, another good sportsman, he played in school sports teams at rugby and cricket. I honestly believe that if Edmund had put his mind to it, that he could have been a first-class professional sportsman. He did play rugby league for a successful amateur team for many years. After leaving school, Edmund went to work for a lighting company, Endura Lamps. He then started work as a driver's mate. The company that he was working for put him through his HGV licence and he had a stint as a long-distance lorry driver.

He later worked with Dave, the husband of Sharon, my daughter, as a double window glazing installer. He stopped working for about three years, travelling between the UK and Spain. When he settled back in the UK he became a taxi driver, his taxi is adapted for wheelchair users, and some of his customers are handicapped children, for whom he would do the school run. Sadly, he lost Karen, the mother of his children, in 2003. Edmund also has three children, Natalie, Keeley and Darryl.

Edmund had his own brush with death. In bed one night he started to hallucinate, then his kidneys started to fail. He was rushed to hospital, but the doctors could not work out what was wrong with him. It turned out that snake venom had got into his system through a cut on his hand after he had touched the outside of a glass case which contained a snake at a local pet store. After a lot of questioning at the hospital, the doctors worked out the problem and Edmund made a full recovery.

Maxine, my second daughter, like all my girls, loves to dance and have a good time and socialise. Her first job was a Saturday job in a bakery, she then had various temporary office jobs like data input and helping with mortgages at a building society. She now works in HR for the Valuation Office Agency, part of HMRC. She married her long-time partner Dougie in 2018. As luck would have it my sister Mel was in England at the time and was able to attend Maxine's wedding party. Maxine has one daughter Lisa.

Sharon comes next. At junior school Sharon took part in Scottish country dancing and took part in a Children's Day festival which was at one time an annual event in Leeds. At thirteen she worked part time with her mother at a café in Leeds, at fifteen she went to work at another café before going to work for a utilities company. She was the first of my daughters to get married, Dave was the lucky man. After leaving that utilities company she helped to run her husband's company for a few years, she now works as a team leader for a large bakery company. She and Dave are now divorced, but they remained friends. She has two children, Gaynor and Aron. Sharon contracted Hodgkin's Disease in 1993 which is a form of cancer. Thankfully, after treatment she made a full recovery.

Next there is Diane. Diane was quite poorly as a child and spent some of her early years in hospital. Thankfully she overcame her illness and was completely healthy by the time she started school. After leaving school she had a couple of part time jobs before moving to Jersey, one of the Channel Islands to work in a hotel. She returned to Leeds after a few years in Jersey and trained as a career's advisor, helping young people to build skills, create a CV and find work or go onto further education.

She then moved to working in prisons, helping prisoners to get back into education. Always studious, Diane took a university course called Celta, which would allow her to teach English as a foreign language. She completed a B.A. Honours Degree in English and Media Studies in 1999. She has worked in various countries around the world teaching English, the last six years in the Middle East. Diane has one child, Dane.

Last but not least is Paula, she had various jobs when she left school. She worked as a croupier in various casinos around the world and on cruise ships. Paula obtained a joint B.A. Honours degree in English and Social Policy. She now works for a charity in Leeds that delivers transformational services to adults, children, young people, and families. She was married to Liam, but sadly that ended up in a separation. She is now in a relationship with a nice man, called Andrew. She has one daughter, Ashleigh.

The family does not end there, at the last count I have sixteen grandchildren, twenty-five great-grandchildren and one great, great grandchild. The family has even moved down under. Laraine's son Ryan moved to Australia a few years ago and started an Aussie branch of the family.

The family tree, as it is at the moment is on the next page.

To say that I'm proud of my children is an understatement. Watching them grow up, with their age differences and their different styles of fashion and different tastes in music, they unwittingly always kept me up to date with all the latest trends. I may not have liked it all, but it was all interesting. I still talk to all of my children and, fortunately, they talk to me too. I don't recall ever falling out with any of them.

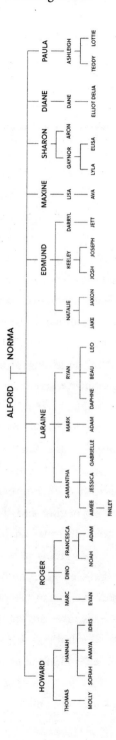

Chapter Twenty-Two

I apologise for the digression. I am very proud of my children but have only written about them incidentally in this book. I will get back to my life. You may think that the years of note are over as I start writing about the lead-up to the new millennium. However, that isn't the view I've taken in my latter years.

In 1998, 50 years after the arrival of HMT *Empire Windrush* in Tilbury, Leeds City Council held a dinner to celebrate the event. I, along with other West Indians who had been invited, went to Leeds Town Hall for the event. My family only found out by accident that the event was taking place. I didn't mention it as I didn't think they'd be interested in the celebrations. My daughter Paula happened to be in Leeds Town Hall attending another function when she bumped into me.

I explained what was happening and she informed the rest of the family. To my surprise they did take an interest. Over the next few weeks, I was the subject of an article in the local paper and appeared on the local TV current affairs programme *Calendar*. I, along with Glen English, another ex-RAF West Indian veteran, went around schools in the Chapeltown area of Leeds, to relate our stories of life in the UK for the early arrivals from the West Indies. I was also interviewed for a couple of books regarding the *Windrush* and appeared in a BBC documentary about the *Windrush*.

Over the years I had told my children that I came to the UK in

1948. However, I don't think I ever mentioned the name of the ship or its importance. I always had the impression that my children were too English and had no interest in Jamaica. I suppose that was my fault, I never spoke about my life in Jamaica to my children, to us Jamaicans moving to the UK there was not much of a cultural difference. We spoke the same language, albeit with an accent, we had the same education system, the only real difference at this time between the UK and Jamaica was the weather, the music and the food.

At this time in the late '90s none of the family had been to Jamaica. I am aware now that it is not because they did not want to go but because they simply could not afford to go at the time. Most of them have been since and are planning to go again in the future. At this moment in time my children and I have never been in Jamaica at the same time. My one big dream is for me to have a big win on the lottery so that I can charter a plane and take the whole of the UK family to the land of my birth. I remember them celebrating with me when Jamaica gained independence, and Howard has always shown interest in any news concerning Jamaica. He has always followed the West Indian cricket team, through thick and thin, and would often go to Headingley to watch a test match when the Windies were playing there.

I didn't appear in the news for a while after that, which was fine by me. I saw my children when I could, travelled when possible and just quietly enjoyed my life with Jean. That all came to a halt in 2005 when Jean was diagnosed with cancer. Everything seemed to stand still then. The initial treatment seemed to be working well, but in 2007 the cancer came back worse than ever. Then in early 2007, Norma suffered her first stroke and in March Roger had a massive heart attack and passed away. In August the same year, Jean lost her battle with cancer. To say it was the worst year the family ever had is a bit of an understatement. It was the lowest point of my life and I don't know what I would have done if my children had not been there for me.

With Jean's passing I made the decision to see more of my family in the States and back in Jamaica. For the next few years around Christmas and the New Year, I would go to New York, travel to Cleveland and to Houston, any place that I had family, including, of course, Jamaica. Altogether I spent around three months away. Sometimes while I was in America, I would accompany Fitz, my niece Georgia's husband, on his travels. Fitz was a long-distance lorry driver and drove one of those big rigs, it was a great way for me to see the country.

In December 2013, Norma died. She had become housebound in the years prior after a series of strokes. I reached out to her a few times over the years, in an attempt to become friends with her again, but she did not want to speak to me. I was in America when she passed away and I know that the children made sure that she had a good send off. She was so well loved that on the day of the funeral there were not enough seats in the crematorium for everyone.

In 2014, I had decided to stop going to the States in winter and started to go in the summer. With so many children, grandchildren, and great-grandchildren, I told the children that I was not going to buy any Christmas presents but would like to book a room in a pub or a restaurant and invite all the family for a meal and it is something we have regularly done since then. My family in the States were now starting to have reunions in Jamaica in the summer, so it made more sense for me to change my dates.

In 2016 I was invited to appear on the BBC TV show, *Real Lives Reunited*. This show brought together people who had been on the *Windrush*. I was reunited with three other passengers: Sam King, the Windrush Foundation founder, a young lady named Dorinda, who was only eighteen months old when she sailed to the UK on the *Windrush* with her family, and one of the crew, Peter Dielhenn, who was a cook on the ship.

There was a reception for us at the High Commissioner's residence in London, and a trip to Tilbury Docks, where we were interviewed about the journey and our time in the UK. My daughter, Sharon, accompanied me for that show and, a couple of years later, another producer from the BBC got in touch with Sharon to ask if I would be available to do another show down at Tilbury Docks and if she would be able to accompany me. That show was *Flog It*; they were having their antique appraisals in the main hall at Tilbury Docks and the history segment of the show wanted to do an interview with someone who had been on the *Windrush*. Sharon was unable to get time off from work, so she asked Howard, who had now retired, to go with me.

We travelled down to London on the train and then on to Tilbury to meet the production team. The BBC had arranged for a taxi to pick us up from Tilbury train station to take us to the hotel, but it never turned up. After a few phone calls, the producer of the show arranged to meet up with us at Tilbury Station to take us to the hotel. They knew my age and when they turned up and were expecting to find someone with a walking stick or Zimmer frame. When the car turned up, I ran across the road to meet them, which took the production team by surprise for me being so spritely.

That evening after the meal, the producer took us for a couple of drinks in the bar and talked us through the procedure for filming the next day. I was then able to keep them entertained for a few hours with some of my stories. A couple of rums and I'm anybody's.

The next day we were taken to Tilbury Docks where we met Paul Martin the presenter of *Flog It*. Filming took place on one of the docks overlooking the River Thames. Paul asked me about arriving in England on the *Windrush* and what I did once we had docked. He then asked Howard of his thoughts on the Windrush generation, who said how proud he was of not just me but of that generation of West Indians who had the courage to leave their homeland, first for some of us to come to a war zone and then to come back a couple of years later to start afresh in a new country. We then had a tour of the docks and arrival hall, before setting off back to Leeds. Little did we know at the time what was about to happen.

Chapter Twenty-Three

At the beginning of 2018 I had heard that there was going to be some form of celebration for the 70th anniversary for the arrival of the *Empire Windrush*, I did not realise at the time just how big it was going to be.

It all started for me with the Leeds based dance company Phoenix Dance Theatre, who were putting on a new dance based on the arrival of the *Windrush*. Sharon Watson, the dance director, was inspired by the stories her mother had told her about what life was like when she first arrived in this country from Jamaica. Sharon got in touch with the Windrush Foundation to ask if they knew of anyone who lived in the Leeds area who had been on the *Windrush*. Arthur Torrington, from the Windrush Foundation, passed on my phone number to Sharon, and she came to my home to have a talk with me about my experience on the *Windrush*. The BBC heard about the project and did a feature on the dance, which aired on the morning news. Sharon was interviewed about the dance and a BBC reporter and film crew came to the house to interview me. I was asked questions about my life again and I showed them my photo album, which has some photos of my early life in the UK.

I had not told any of the family that I had been interviewed. They were surprised when I popped up on the *BBC Breakfast* news show. The interview and especially the photo album sparked a lot of interest. Sharon got in touch with me to say that she was getting emails and phone calls from various parties asking to talk to me. I do not have email or that kind of thing, so I asked her if she would get in touch with Howard. Sharon then got in touch with Howard and they arranged for me to be interviewed at my home. Howard came to see me about it and I said, 'bring it on.' So he set up a couple of interviews for me at my home. If I had known how things were going to take off like they did, I would have started to charge a fee.

One of the first interviews was with Audrey Dewjee, who was doing an article about West Indian airmen who had done their basic training in Yorkshire. Audrey first spoke to me over the phone and arranged to see me at my home. We had a good long talk about my time in Filey.

Then Mr Colin Grant (an author from London), the Geraldine Connor Foundation (they do educational projects for the West Indian community in the Yorkshire area, bringing people together through arts and culture) and Bill Hern (who works alongside Arthur Torrington of the Windrush Foundation) interviewed me. I was just going over the same stories, but thanks to some in depth questions I was beginning to recall more events that had occurred in my life.

I was then asked by Sharon at Phoenix if I would like to meet the dancers and to attend a rehearsal. Howard and I went along to the Northern Dance theatre building to watch the rehearsal. I then did a short video interview for them. Soon afterwards Howard, his wife Helen and I were invited to the opening night. A couple of my daughters and granddaughters also attended.

On the opening night, I was interviewed by the two local Yorkshire news and current affair programs, *Look North* and *Calendar*. The Lord Mayor of Leeds and various local celebrities also attended that first night, and I was surprised that most people were interested in me. The dance was a big success and went on a sold-out tour of England and Europe.

The next person to get in touch was Jim Grover. Jim was in the process of setting up a photo exhibition in London called *Windrush:*

Portrait of a Generation. Jim had been taking photos of West Indians in his local community of Clapham and had wanted to meet someone who had been on the *Windrush* and had seen me on the BBC news. He got in touch with Sharon from Phoenix Dance, who again put him in touch with Howard. He came to see me, and we got on well. At the end of the interview he arranged to come back again and take some portrait photos for his exhibition. There were then some more newspaper and radio interviews. I was happy to talk to them all about my time in the RAF, the journey on the *Windrush* and my life in the UK.

Another interview was with Everton Wright and Ionie Richards from Eve Wright Studios in Essex. The duo were artists doing an exhibition called Caribbean TakeAway Café, a collection of stories, interviews, and photos from West Indian elders. I was invited to attend the exhibition. Unfortunately, it was at the same time as the main Windrush celebrations were taking place and I was unable to find the time to get over to Essex.

Around the beginning of June, my daughter Paula received a request from a person she knew at the NHS to attend an awards ceremony for the NHS in Manchester; the NHS were celebrating 70 years of its existence. I went with Howard and Paula, we were taken aback by the scale of the event. We were expecting a small gathering, but it turned out to be one of the main events in the NHS anniversary calendar.

On arrival we were welcomed by Yvonne Coghill CBE, who explained to us that I was to receive an award from the NHS. We were led to the top table and sat alongside various VIPs from the NHS and Mr Andy Burnham, the mayor of Manchester. To say Howard, Paula and I felt a little out of place was an understatement. After the meal, there were a few speeches, then the awards were handed out and I was one of the first to receive one. I was surprised, but proud to receive this award on behalf of the Windrush generation.

Lord Victor Adebowale, who was presenting the awards, called me up on to the stage to receive my award. I asked Howard and Paula to go up to the stage with me. Paula did not want to, so she took some photos of me on stage. Howard did accompany me but stood a few feet behind me.

When my name was called out there was some music playing. I got up and halfway to the stage, I can't remember what tune was playing, I started to do a little jig, which brought a large cheer. Lord Victor then presented me with a beautiful, engraved glass vase. Once all the awards had been presented there was a disco, and I was soon up and dancing. As the event was only in Manchester we had decided not to stay over. Midnight came and went and the party was still going. It was time to set off back home to Leeds, but I was having such a good time dancing, surrounded by six women, that Howard had to come and drag me from the dance floor (how times change).

The inscription on the vase says.

70

YEARS

OF THE NHS

1948-2018

WINDRUSH AWARDS 2018

MR ALFORD GARDNER

By accident I now appeared to have become the figure head for the Windrush generation. When I boarded the ship all those years ago, I never could have predicted this. I am immensely proud to be recognised in this way. My fellow passengers and I came to help when the UK needed help, to rebuild the infrastructure, to work on the railways, the buses, the postal service and to work in the factories. This time we were not forced to do it like our African ancestors, who were taken to the West Indies and the Americas by force. We helped to put the 'Great' back into Great Britain.

Jim Grover invited Howard (Howard had now become my unofficial PA), his wife Helen and I to the opening of his exhibition at the gallery@

oxo on the South Bank, London. We had an amazing night, with many of the people who had taken part in the production of Jim's book also attending the show and I appeared to be on my way to becoming a bit of a star. Jim and I were asked by the BBC to appear on the Radio 4 *Today* program, mainly to talk about the exhibition, but questions were also asked about the Windrush scandal. Jim and I answered the questions with ease. Towards the end of the interview, I was asked what kept me going, and, in my best Barry White voice, I said 'lurrve', which brought much laughter in the studio and a cringe from Howard who was watching the interview.

Jim and Ruth really looked after us, with first class travel on our journeys to London and putting us up at the Royal Horseguards Hotel. They would take us out for a nice meal when the exhibition closed on an evening. For the next few days, we all spent time at the exhibition. I did a couple of more interviews for the local papers and for BBC Radio London. I also met a young lady, Amelia Gentlemen, a reporter from *The Guardian* newspaper, who asked if she could come and visit me in Leeds to do an interview. She was doing an article on the Windrush scandal, and she later wrote a book about it, *The Windrush Betrayal*. I also did an interview with Tradewinds, a company run by a nice couple, Janet and Mandingo. Things were going so well for Jim that he asked if it was possible for us to return the next weekend. Howard was unavailable so Paula went with me.

On Saturday, Paula managed to get some tickets for the show *Dreamgirls*, I really enjoyed it. The young men in the show reminded me of the time when I was young and fit and could dance.

It was another very successful weekend with me at Jim's exhibition. He asked me if I could attend for the final weekend, I went with Howard. Over the three weekends that I was there, I became quite the star. It was strange for me to be approached by people when walking about, all saying that they had just been to the exhibition and seen the photos.

I spent most of the time sat near the entrance of the gallery. One of my photos was one of the first ones you saw when you entered the exhibition. People would come into the exhibition, look at the photos, see me sitting there and remark to their friends, 'that is the man in the photo.' I would always say, 'it wasn't me, I didn't say it, it's what the man said, it wasn't me.' Many of the visitors would come and talk to me, take selfies with me. One young lady came to talk to me; she had come to see the man who had said 'lurrve' on the radio.

I must be on hundreds of phones, and when people were taking their photos, I would say, 'that's another camera wrecked,' and start to laugh. At the exhibition, people of all races, both young and old, were enjoying it, that was my favourite part of it all. For the seventeen days of the exhibition Jim set a record for the gallery@oxo with 12,831 visitors passing through the door. The visitor book had some amazing comments in it, with only a handful of negative comments.

I don't want to get too political, that's not me, but about the time of the build up to the Windrush commemorative events, the immigration scandal which affected mainly the second generation of Caribbean people in the UK became nationally known. This has made me so angry; we know that there are some illegal immigrants in the country, but the government of the day appeared to go after the easiest targets. Quite a few people of West Indian origin were wrongly accused of being in the country illegally, some had already been deported, many had lost jobs and had even been refused NHS care.

Some were even locked up in detention centres just waiting to be thrown out of the country. These people had been in Britain for decades, they had wives and children, they had been paying tax and national insurance, some had even served in the armed forces, but due to new Home Office rules, when their history was checked there was no evidence of them arriving in the country. Most of these people were children who had arrived in the UK with their parents in the '50s and '60s, but due to poor administration, these children had not been registered as arriving in the country.

This is not the kind of thing to happen in a civilised country. After a huge media campaign for justice, the British government admitted their mistake, apologised and offered financial compensation to everyone who had been affected. The incident became known as the 'Windrush scandal'. Even now some of these people are still waiting for their cases to be resolved, and the longer this situation goes on, the more some of these people will pass away while never getting the compensation and justice they are entitled to.

Chapter Twenty-Four

Back in Leeds, I was invited, along with Howard, to do an interview on the Radio 5 Live *Steve Nolan Show* at the BBC studio in Leeds. The interview was also with Michael King, the son of the late Sam King, and Sam King's granddaughter, who were in the studio in London. We discussed racism and the Windrush scandal. Now, when I think back to that radio interview, I don't think it was my finest hour. When I was asked the question about racism, I simply said that, 'I had no problem,' but could not elaborate on why I had no problem. It must have been nerves that night.

The next thing I heard was that there was to be a service of celebration, Spirit of Windrush, to be held at Westminster Abbey on June 22nd. Along with other surviving people from the *Empire Windrush*, I was to be invited. Now I know that there are not many of us left and the only other Windrush survivor I can remember meeting that day was Mr John Richards.

Howard then received a call from Paulette Simpson of *The Voice* newspaper, a paper dedicated to championing diversity. He learned that a few days before the service at Westminster Abbey, the speaker of the House of Commons was to hold a reception in his office in the Houses of Parliament on June 19th. I went with Howard to the reception, where we met the Speaker of the House, Mr John Bercow, and other dignitaries, including the High CCommissioner of Barbados, Mr H. E. Guy Hewitt and Baroness Floella Benjamin, along with the ex-hurdler and now sports commentator Colin Jackson.

I still find it hard to believe that I, a Jamaican country boy, was mixing it with MPs and members of the House of Lords. I wish that I could remember the names of all the people that I met that day.

Howard, his wife Helen, and I set off to attend the Westminster service on June 21st, with the service being held the next day. On the train journey Howard received more emails, one was from the Windrush Foundation, Channel 5 News had requested an interview with me, which I did in a pub near to Kings Cross station.

Howard had to turn down a request from *The One Show* and *BBC Morning News*, who both wanted to do an interview with me on the morning of June 22nd at Tilbury Docks, unfortunately we just did not have the time. Another request then came from the Prime Minister's office, we had been invited to a reception at Number 10 to be held after the service at Westminster Abbey. They needed the names of all who were accompanying me. I also found out that the 22nd of June would from now on be called Windrush Day.

On our arrival at the Abbey, there was a long queue of people waiting to get in. A young lady from the production company Twenty Twenty, the documentary company run by author and TV presenter David Olusoga, approached me for an interview. They were doing a documentary called *The Unwanted: The Secret Windrush Files,* which was not only about the Windrush scandal, but also about how the government at the time set about making a hostile environment for the West Indian settlers. I was not aware of this. This appeared to me to be more apparent in London, rather than in the other cities. Howard gave the young lady his email address, I did the interview for them at my house later that year.

The queue outside the Abbey had grown since we'd stopped to chat with the young lady. Howard suggested we had better get in the queue, but I insisted we walk straight to the front. Fortunately, we'd met one of the organisers of the service, Dr Elizabeth Henry, at the gallery@oxo. She saw us and helped us bypass the queue. As we walked to the entrance there were quite a few reporters and TV cameras, I was called over and asked a couple of questions, some about the event and some regarding the Windrush scandal. Just before I went into the Abbey, I met another man who was on the *Windrush*, Mr John Richards. We had a little chat before a reporter from ITV News interviewed us.

When we went into the Abbey there was a steel band playing the hymn 'Amazing Grace' to welcome the guests and during the event a group of actors were recounting the story of the arrival of the *Windrush* at Tilbury. The Kingdom Choir sang a new song that had been commissioned for the service called 'Hold My Hand'. The Kingdom Choir, for those who are not aware, are the choir who sang at the wedding of Prince Harry and Meghan Markle.

As we sat waiting for everyone to arrive, suddenly a cheer went up. At the time I did not know what was happening. I later found out that Baroness Floella Benjamin had started to do a little jig as she walked up the aisle. If I had known, I would have gone to join her.

In the Abbey we were shown to our seats, which was in the part of the Abbey called the Quire, (what people up north would call the 'posh seats'). I had seen the Abbey on TV before, but I never realised just how big the place was. The service was an amazing event and was attended by Prime Minister Theresa May and politicians from both sides of Parliament and from across the Caribbean. There were also about 2000 guests, mainly from the Caribbean community.

When we left the service, we met up with Sharon from Phoenix Dance, she had not been able to sit with us in the Abbey, and we walked down to Downing Street. Howard had informed me the night before that to enter Downing Street we would all need some type of photo ID and he had told me to bring my passport. On arriving at the gate, we were met by the security staff (men with guns). They checked to make sure that our names were on the list, they then asked for ID. Both Howard and Helen had theirs and showed the security their passports, I started to check my pockets for my passport and was not able to locate it. The policeman standing with a sub-machine looked at me as I was searching for my passport and said to me, 'you look harmless enough, get in.' As we walked through the gate I reached into another pocket and pulled out my passport, I knew I had it.

As we approached the door of 10 Downing Street the door opened like magic like you see on TV by the doorman. He must stand there all day just looking out of the window to see who is approaching the door. I had a look around the room, but I couldn't see any cameras or CCTV. We were asked to leave our mobile phones in security in the lobby and were then escorted to the gardens at the back of the house. I never realised that the garden was that large.

Once outside in the garden I was approached by the parliamentary official Nero, he was the person who had been in touch with Howard regarding our invite. He asked us to stand near the back door so that when the Prime Minister arrived, he could introduce us. When she came into the garden, Nero brought her over, we shook hands and had a short conversation, she was then introduced to Howard and Helen and also to Sharon Watson. We met other leading government figures that night. I can't remember all of them, but I know one was Sajid Javid.

The PM made a pleasant speech about the Windrush generation and what they had done for the country, adding complimentary things about me. In one of my interviews, I had been asked if I would change anything in my life and I replied that, 'I would not change one damned thing,' Mrs May repeated that quote in her speech.

When we left Downing Street, we went with Sharon Watson to Tilbury Docks, where the Phoenix Dance theatre were doing a performance of their Windrush dance. There was a party going on in the arrival hall, and we were welcomed by a young lady who got us a table and brought us tea and something to eat. Around the room were TV screens showing programs that had been made about the *Windrush* over the years. We then went through to another hall to watch the dance.

After watching the performance we travelled back to London by boat. That was a pleasant boat ride, the sun was shining and the bar was open, not that I wanted a drink. At the Tilbury dance performance there were some NHS staff, some of whom I had danced with at their Manchester event a few weeks earlier. It was the first time that I had travelled by boat into London from the docks. It had been a long enjoyable day. On the train back to the hotel, Howard, Helen and I realised that we had not had a proper meal all day. We decided to go to the first place we saw once we got off the train. KFC never tasted so good.

On the way home the next day, Howard mentioned that I was looking tired. I would not admit it, but the travelling over the last few weeks was starting to take its toll on me. Howard checked his diary, we had no other functions to attend, so he suggested that I go see our family in the States. I agreed and was on my way within a few days.

I first went to New York to meet up with family there, before a few of us flew out to Jamaica. Apparently I was becoming a little bit of a celebrity in my own country. I was invited to the Jamaican Independence Day celebrations in Kingston where I met the Jamaican Prime Minister. I also presented a polo shirt which I had made for myself for the 1998 Windrush celebrations to the National Library of Jamaica. I also had a Q&A with an invited audience.

I returned from the trip to the USA and Jamaica in September, only for Howard to inform me that we had been invited to another awards event, the National Windrush Star Awards in Nottingham. The event was held at the Nottingham Belfry and we had another fantastic night with me dancing the night away as usual.

I did a couple of interviews the day after and, as usual, people wanted to talk to me and have selfies taken with me.

In December 2018, Arthur Torrington invited me to an event

at Lambeth Town Hall to celebrate the launching of the book, *The Windrush 70, Pioneers and Champions.* Arthur is the co-founder and Director of the Windrush Foundation, which he and the late Sam King established. The Foundation is a fantastic organisation, which keeps the stories and the history of the Windrush generation alive. As a charity it does a lot of work for the Caribbean community. Awards were given to Windrush pioneers like myself, also for my late brother Gladstone. Howard collected Gladstone's award and sent it to my nephew Errol. Fellow RAF WWII serviceman Mr Allan Charles Wilmot, age 93, was also there and received his award.

The book itself is a collection of photos and profiles of 70 outstanding Caribbean men and women who have helped shape the country whether through working in the factories or in the NHS or through entertainment in TV, film, or the arts. We again met Baroness Floella Benjamin.

We also attended another showing of the Windrush dance at Leeds University by the Phoenix Dance Theatre, which was followed by a Q&A with the audience. The questions were more political and I was not sure how to answer, so I passed them on to the younger members of the panel.

After all the excitement of 2018, 2019 got off to a slow start for me. We had a big do for my 93rd birthday, which I really enjoyed. Nearly all the family was there and Jim Grover came up from London to join the party. Then in April, Howard received an email from a Fran Miller, who worked for the National Theatre. They were doing a production of Andrea Levy's acclaimed novel *Small Island*. A member of the production team had met me at the gallery@oxo Windrush exhibition and thought it would be a good idea to invite me to a rehearsal and meet the cast. One of the characters in Levy's book, Gilbert, joined the RAF during World War II, after being demobbed he returned to Jamaica only to return to the UK on the *Windrush*.

Howard and I agreed to a Q&A with the cast, which was a great experience. We were also given a tour of the theatre. Then I did a video interview for them which can be found on YouTube. We were then invited to the press viewing of the show, which was another amazing night. There were a lot of famous people from stage and screen attending the show, but I don't really watch a lot of TV or films and did not know exactly who some of the stars were. Howard got a bit excited; he was a big fan of some TV show called *Game of Thrones*, and one of the stars of the show was at the reception, and Howard managed to get a photo taken with him.

We almost did not make it to the show. Howard had told me to meet him outside the Boots store on the concourse at Leeds train station. I arrived at 12.30 sharp. I was looking around for Howard when I bumped into my great granddaughters Aimee and Jessica, they were getting a train to Manchester airport on their way on holiday. I asked them if they had seen Howard, but they had not. I decided to phone Howard when I realised that I had forgotten my mobile phone. My granddaughters phoned their mother, who then phoned Howard. Howard had said to meet at 13.30 and I'd gotten mixed up. When I found out I was an hour early I realised I had time to rush back home and pick up my mobile phone.

How wrong I was. I just missed the first bus back to Leeds and the next one never turned up. I arrived back at the train station with not even two minutes to spare. Howard was pacing up and down the concourse. When he saw me he grabbed my case, and we ran to the ticket gate. I thought that he was going to make me vault the ticket barrier, but he managed to use his ticket to open it.

We jumped on the train with about ten seconds to spare and I couldn't help but smile. That incident brought back a memory. Every Saturday I would go to Leeds Market at about 5 o'clock and buy reduced meat, fruit and veg. I would drag Howard, eleven years old at the time, along, whether he liked it or not. We were on our way back to the bus station, when I saw our bus just pulling away. 'Run!' I shouted to Howard, we both set off laden with bags.

The bus was getting to the exit of the station and was gathering speed, but we were determined. We kept running and managed to jump onto the back of the bus. We made our way up to the top deck and sat down, the conductor came to take our fare. He had been watching us, as was half of the bus.

'I can understand you running and jumping like that with your wife to catch the bus, but not with your lad' he said, which brought a smile to some of the passengers. I was too out of breath to reply. It took about 60 years, but I think Howard was getting his own back by making me run for the train.

On 23 June 2019, the Caribbean Cricket Club that I helped establish in Leeds in 1948 invited me to a Windrush Day celebration. I was presented with the current Caribbean Cricket Club shirt and a silver plate by the legendary cricketer-turned-umpire Mr John Holder. I knew that I was going to be presented with the shirt, so I turned up in my old white cricket trousers, well more of a cream now. There was a mini tournament between four teams being played that day on a round robin basis. It was not the best day for cricket with a strong cold breeze blowing across the ground. Thankfully I wasn't asked to play, but I did manage a game of dominoes.

Howard and Helen were there along with Laraine and Paula, plus a couple of granddaughters and great granddaughters. The presentation was held in the pavilion before the final game, and I was immensely proud to receive the gifts on behalf of the Windrush generation from my old club.

In July 2019, the American and Jamaican side of the family were organising a Gardner reunion in Jamaica, the reason being to help renovate the Gardner family home Sunnyside Cottage. The English side were invited and Howard, his wife Helen and Paula looked into the possibility of going over to the reunion, but after checking the prices of flights and hotels, realised that it was too expensive and, unfortunately, they had to give it a miss.

This was another occasion that I almost missed, the flight had been booked for me July 10th, to take off at 10.30am. Unfortunately I left home far later than I should have, thinking that I had plenty of time to check in (Jamaican timing again). When I arrived at the airport I went to the wrong terminal. By the time I arrived at the correct terminal the gate was closed. I argued with the security, saying that they were still calling people to board the plane. I was not allowed to board because my bags had not been checked in. I phoned Howard to let him know what had happened and returned home to Leeds. Another flight was arranged, and I flew out on Sunday July 12th. My daughter Paula accompanied me to the airport and made sure that I was there in plenty of time to check in.

My niece Georgia was due to meet me at the airport in New York, but on arriving I decided to make my own way to Georgia's house without telling anyone. This caused a bit of panic in New York, and Howard got a frantic phone call from Georgia asking if I had made my flight. I was eventually found and, after a couple of days in New York, the American side of the family took a flight to Montego Bay and then on to Sunnyside Cottage, where we did some restoration work, some painting and tidying up the garden.

After a couple of weeks in Jamaica, I returned to the USA and stayed in Cleveland with my sister, before returning to New York for the rest of my stay. The week before I was due to return home, I could not find my details for my return flight. I asked Georgia to get in touch with Kim (the daughter in law of my late partner Jean). She was the person who had organised my trip, but she happened to be on holiday in Turkey.

After a few phone calls, texts, and emails we managed to get all the details for my return flight. When I received the details, I noticed that I was booked on a Thomas Cook flight. At the time of receiving the flight details, Thomas Cook were trying to secure a loan, hoping to stay in business, but two days later the company went into liquidation, leaving about 150,000 passengers stranded in various parts of the world, including me, wondering on how we were going to get home.

With Kim still on holiday, Howard and Paula had to work out how to get me home. Fortunately, the CAA (Civil Aviation Authority) set up a website for stranded passengers where they put details of phone numbers for various airlines, so both Howard and Paula went about trying to arrange a flight to get me home.

They needed to get me a flight home to Manchester. Paula at first arranged a flight on BA to Heathrow. I was ok with that, but Paula was not happy about it and asked Howard if he could get in touch with BA to try and change the flight. He phoned BA, only to be told they only did flights to Heathrow. I informed Paula, she asked if he had tried Virgin, he had not because he believed that they only flew to Gatwick and Heathrow, but Paula then got in touch with Virgin and was able to get me a flight into Manchester. Howard picked me up from the airport and I was happy to be back in the UK and to get back to my bingo.

Things went quiet again for a while until I was contacted by Adina Campbell from the BBC, she had already done a couple of interviews with me, one at the West Indian Centre in Leeds, where grandchildren and great-grandchildren asked me a few questions about my life in the UK, this was shown on the late *BBC News*. They asked if I was available to meet up with Mr John Richards, the other *Windrush* passenger to talk about our relative experiences in the UK. It was for a documentary on immigration. Mr Richards lived in London and had worked for British Rail until his retirement.

Howard and I travelled down to London on 22 October 2019 with a producer from the BBC. We were met by the producer, Joanna, at Leeds City train station, along with a cameraman who filmed me walking down the platform, getting on to the train and then answering a few questions whilst I was sat on the train. On arriving at Kings Cross Station we were met by Adina and another film crew, where they did some more filming of me getting off the train before setting off to Mr Richards' home in north-west London, where we were filmed having a conversation talking about our respective lives.

There was to be a new showing of Jim Grover's exhibition *Windrush: Portrait of a Generation* being shown at the newly refurbished Fairfield Hall in Croydon on 26 October 2019. Jim asked me if I would be happy to make a guest appearance. Howard and I travelled down the day before. Now I always leave travel arrangements to Howard, he gets all the details and I just do what I'm told. When we arrived at King's Cross, Howard said that we had to go over to St Pancras to catch the train to Croydon.

Now I have to admit that Howard is quite good at finding the correct platforms, but this time he had some trouble. After about ten minutes walking up and down, looking at different signposts he realised that we were on the wrong level, but he got us there in the end. We arrived at Croydon around about five in the evening, got settled in our hotel, and Howard took me for my first ever Nando's meal. Now I don't know much about Nando's, but it was the first time that I have seen a bouncer on the door to a restaurant and then having to use plastic knives and forks.

When Howard and I arrived at Fairfield Hall, we were met by author and playwright Weekes Baptiste, who was going to be asking me questions. We met up with Jim and Ruth, they had set up the exhibition at one side of the hall.

A stage had been set up with two chairs on it, with the audience sat in front of them, it was a bit like BBC's *Question Time*. Mr Baptiste started the ball rolling, by asking me about my early life in Jamaica, the audience soon started to get involved. I was asked about my time in the RAF, it's strange when you mention being in the RAF people automatically think that you flew Spitfires or bombers. One person asked me, 'did I like flying a plane?' I've never flown a plane, but I'm sure I would have enjoyed it.

I was asked again about being on the *Windrush* and what life was like in the UK in the '50s. The audience had a mixed age group, and nationalities. One chap came to see me. I believe he was Romanian; he was fascinated by my story, and we spoke for about half an hour. Once the actual event was finished, Jim and I stayed around and mingled with members of the audience, and during the afternoon as people wandered into the exhibition hall they would walk around and look at Jim's exhibition then come and chat to Jim or myself.

In 2019, Susan Pitter of the Jamaica Society in Leeds asked if I would like to do an interview for her new project titled Eulogy, this was a series of photos and stories of Jamaicans who had made their home in Leeds. I did the interview on May 10th, just before I set off on one of my trips to the US.

I was unable to attend the exhibition of the Eulogy project, which was held at the Leeds Art Gallery and proved to be a great success, but I was there for the book launch. Along with Mr Roper, another West Indian ex-RAF serviceman, who, unfortunately, has since passed away, presented a copy of the *Eulogy* book to Leeds City Council.

In 2020, Covid-19 hit the world and, with various lockdowns, put a stop to my bingo and travel. I, like everyone in the country, found this time to be very hard. I live on my own and my own family were not allowed to visit me, I could not visit them, but thanks to technology, we were able to have Zoom calls with family in England and the States. The Zoom calls have been such a success, and both families are getting to know each other, that we now have one on the last Sunday of each month, where we catch up on events on both sides of the pond and celebrate the people who have birthdays in that particular month. Hopefully now that most people are getting their jabs, I should be able to visit the States soon.

The Windrush Foundation also did some very entertaining and informative Zoom events during lockdown on some Windrush passengers. There was one about the singer Mona Baptiste and the calypso singer Harold Phillips. They did one about the history of Black soldiers in the UK going back to when the Romans invaded Britain and they did a show about me, which was quite enjoyable.

Even being in lockdown, things did not stop for me. A BBC producer, working on the popular *Antiques Roadshow*, was doing a special programme on WWII. They got in touch with Howard through Susan

Pitter, to ask if I would do an interview regarding my time in the RAF. I was asked to take any items relating to my time in the Forces. I still had a few papers which I took along to the filming, which was held at Newby Hall in North Yorkshire, and I spoke about the duties I had to do while serving in the RAF. I also spoke about my return on the *Windrush*, and Howard, who was not aware that he was also going to be interviewed, spoke of how proud he was of me and all the other West Indian servicemen who had served in WWII.

To be honest, I never expected when I joined the RAF and then returned to the UK on the *Empire Windrush* that in later years I, along with my fellow West Indians, would be such a part of British history and culture. I have been asked on many occasions if I regret any part of my life, and I always say, 'I would not change one damn thing.'

In 2021, the Rugby League World Cup took place in England, and the Jamaican team qualified for the first time in their history, after beating the USA national side. My granddaughter Natalie does a bit of work for a Mr Alex Simmons, who is doing work for the Jamaican national team. In conversation with Natalie he spoke about getting a Jamaican elder to act as the face of the team. She mentioned me, and they gave me a ring and asked if I was prepared to help out. Of course I said yes, so Alex said that he would be in touch to sort things out at a later date.

Alex got in touch with Howard to arrange a photoshoot with the team and me. I was asked to wear the official team clothes, Farah shirt and trousers, with a pair of Clark shoes. For those who are not aware, Clark shoes are the in-shoes to wear in Jamaica.

I was asked to read a poem in Jamaican patois, which took a few takes. It has been a long time since I have had to speak like that, but I eventually managed it. I then went out onto the rugby pitch at Headingley, where photos were taken of me wearing the team clothes and then some with the team.

A few weeks later I did an interview with Alex, which was part of a documentary Alex was doing for the rugby team.

I was later invited to attend the rugby match where Jamaica was playing Scotland at Post Office Road, Featherstone. This was my first rugby match in years, the game was very close with Jamaica coming from a losing position to draw 30 points each. Mr Levi Roots the TV chef was another special guest of the team and was attending his first ever Rugby League game. Speaking to him after the game he told me that he really enjoyed it.

In February 2022, Howard had a phone call with Paulette Simpson of *The Voice* newspaper, to say that there was to be an event taking place at Waterloo train station on Windrush Day, June 22nd.

It was to be the unveiling of a monument which was an idea of Baroness Floella Benjamin and was to be dedicated to the arrival of those West Indians who arrived in the UK in the fifties and sixties who had passed through Waterloo. Many of these people had sailed to Southampton instead of Tilbury.

Howard told me about the invite but mentioned that he would not be able to attend the unveiling because he had already booked a holiday for that week. So, he asked Paula if she would like to attend with me, to which she said yes if she could arrange time off from work, which she duly did.

As the date got nearer, Howard put Paula in touch with Paulette to sort out travel and accommodation details. Paula asked if it would be okay for my great-granddaughter Gabrielle to travel down with us, to which Paulette said yes.

As usual, things do not always go as planned. A train strike had been organised for the day we were due to travel down to London and Paula did not fancy the idea of driving all that way, so we had to find another way of getting there. The only other way was to fly down, which we did.

We flew from Manchester down to Heathrow, where a car was waiting to take us to our hotel. The driver when meeting us, said to me, 'I don't know whether to bow or salute you, you are quite the celebrity and there are a lot of people wanting to meet you.'

After a peaceful night in the hotel we were picked up and driven to Waterloo Station. When we arrived at Waterloo, we were met by Baroness Benjamin, Michael Gove and Paulette who informed me that Gabrielle and myself would participate in the unveiling. Also there was Mr John Richards, the other Windrush passenger, who I had met a few times in the last few years.

The biggest surprise I got was when the Duke and Duchess of Cambridge arrived, I had not realised how important the event was going to be. Gabrielle and I were introduced to the Duke and Duchess, they both had a few words with us, with Prince William asking me what my secret was to long life. Wish I knew the answer, I could bottle it and make a fortune.

After some speeches, it was time for the unveiling of the monument, so along with the Duke and Duchess of Cambridge, Baroness Benjamin, Gabrielle, some other school children, John, and I we pulled off the sheet to reveal the monument, which was designed by Jamaican artist Basil Watson. The monument depicts a man, woman and child stood on what West Indians know as grips, what everyone else in the world would call a suitcase.

Not to upset anyone, but as I said earlier the monument is really dedicated to the later arrivals from the West Indies, who passed through Waterloo, after sailing into Southampton, and I believe that John and I should have left the unveiling to the young children.

After a few photos were taken beside the monument, we caught a boat to Tilbury Docks to see the art exhibition of Everton Wright, which is on one of the gangways leading to the arrival hall. I was surprised to see a few photos of me on there. There was also the Phoenix Dance Company Windrush dance, which I still enjoy seeing.

After another memorable day we were taken back to Heathrow to catch our plane back to Manchester.

The Leeds Jamaican Society are celebrating the 60th anniversary of Jamaica's independence with a series of events being held at various venues in Leeds, called 'The Out Of Many Festival'. This festival again curated by Susan Pitter is a follow up to the earlier Eulogy exhibition, and is about the second generation of West Indians, those who were born in the UK.

Along with Howard and daughter Laraine, I went to the opening night at the Central Library of Leeds, this part of the festival called 'Rebellion to Romance', and through a series of photos and exhibits showed how music and fashion of the second generation changed over the years.

Susan then invited Howard and I to the 'Road to Trojan', a concert at the Leeds Playhouse, and oh what a night I had. It was the best night I have had in years. It was a history of Jamaican music starting with a type of music called mento, the first type of music that I remember, then going through ska and rocksteady music, then on to reggae. I repeat, oh what a night, I may be 96 years old, and my legs are not as strong as they used to be, but the music got me up and dancing.

Chapter Twenty-Five

That is things up to now. I have had an interesting and varied life and looking forward to seeing what 2023 will bring. The 75th celebrations of the arrival of the *Windrush*, should be another good party. There is also the 75th anniversary of the NHS, and of the formation of the Caribbean Cricket Club.

Yes, 2023 is going to be a good year.

Would I change anything in my life? NO. I have had a beautiful life, I have shared it with two wonderful women, Norma and Jean, brought up a lovely family, I have all those grandchildren, great-grandchildren and one great-great-grandchild, what more could a man want, (apart from winning the lottery)?

The main message that I have for people is to enjoy life, try not to have any regrets and make everyday count.

ONE LOVE

Afterword

As my father has stated in his memoirs, 2018 became another pivotal year in his life. There he was just living his life going to bingo when a phone call and a *BBC Breakfast News* interview changed his life.

It was after that appearance on the news that things started to get serious. This is where I come into it. Dad doesn't do the internet or use a computer, and people were wanting to meet him, so he asked for my help in arranging meetings for him. He had a few interviews with people, this then led onto the invites to various events regarding the *Windrush*. It was at one of these events that someone suggested that a book should be written about his life. At the time I didn't give it much thought, and really who could we get to do it or even publish it.

As my siblings and I were growing up, Dad never spoke much about his life back home in Jamaica. All we knew was that he came to the UK during the war and was in the RAF, then after going back home after the war, returned by ship in 1948. We were never told which ship. It was not until the 50th anniversary of the arrival of the ship the HMT *Empire Windrush* in 1998, that we got to know a little bit more about him, thanks to newspaper articles, a couple of interviews that he did for a couple of books and a TV documentary on the BBC.

The events that he was being invited to were mostly in London and we would travel down by train. This was the first time that we started to spend time together since we used to go to the cricket in the late fifties, early sixties, it was on these journeys that dad started telling me some stories, about him growing up, the people who he played with at school and his school life.

Then he would talk about his RAF days, where he did his training, where he was stationed, the kind of things that he did on leave and where he would go when on leave. At the time I wasn't making any notes or recording the things he was telling me like I should have done, but I have a good memory and I retained most of the things he told me.

The more Dad told me the more I began to realise that there could be a book about his life. I mentioned it to Arthur Torrington of the Windrush Foundation and he thought it was a good idea. Now I have never written a book, I could not even write a full-page composition when I was at school, so the thought of me helping dad to do his biography I found daunting.

Arthur sent me two books, written by Jamaicans, to read. Allan Wilmot's *Now You Know* and Sam King's *Climbing Up The Rough Side Of The Mountain* to give Dad and I an idea of how to start. I began putting things down on the computer, I would print it off and go show dad to make sure that I was on the right track. Then Covid-19 hit the world and with lockdown and restrictions, everything was put on hold.

I kept on writing, trying to remember all the things that he told me on those train journeys. After a while I got to about 17,000 words, and thinking to myself that it was not enough, but was not sure where to go next. Thankfully, lockdown and restrictions were lifted, and I was able to go see Dad and sit down and get some stories.

I sent a draft of what I had written to Arthur to get his thoughts on the things I had written. Thankfully, he was pleased with the work so far and he sent the draft back with comments and suggestions.

Over the last couple of years I have spent more time with Dad than the first 67 years of my life. I have learnt about his childhood, my grandparents, my aunties and uncle, his life in the RAF and the things he got up to. The things that he got up to once he left the RAF, how he met my mother and the journey on the *Windrush* back to the UK.

What I learnt the most from Dad's story and the research that I did is that it is that the men of the islands of the Caribbean volunteered to join the Forces. They did not have to leave the warm Caribbean seas for the cold of the North Sea. They did not know how the war would turn out, they came to help the Mother Country, in her hour of need.

After the war most of the men went back to their islands, only to return after hearing that the Mother Country needed help in rebuilding the country. They came back to a country to find that they were needed but not wanted. Dad's story tells the struggles of the men who came to the UK to help, not once but twice within a few years.

This book is Dad's words, I just helped him to put it all down on paper.

I hope that you enjoyed it.

Howard Gardner

Acknowledgements

We would like to thank Mr Arthur Torrington of the Windrush Foundation for his help in the creation of this book. We would also like to thank the Jacaranda staff for all of their work bringing the book to life.

About the Authors

Alford Dalrymple Gardner

Born in 1926 in Kingston, Jamaica, Alford Gardner first came to England in 1944 to support the war effort, serving in the RAF. After a brief stay back in Jamaica, he decided to return to England to help to rebuild the country. He boarded the HMT *Empire Windrush* intending to build a life in the country he once called home. Despite a less than accommodating welcome back, he persisted and succeeded in forging a better life for his family.

Now 97 and twice widowed, Alford spends all his leisure time at the bingo hall. When not playing bingo, he can be found watching sports or spending time with his family. A much fuller sense of Alford's life is conveyed in his autobiography: Finding Home.

Howard Gardner

Howard Gardner, not the American psychologist, but a retired engineer from Leeds. Taking after his father, Howard is a big sports fan, especially rugby league and supports Leeds Rhinos. He also follows Leeds United, Yorkshire Cricket team and the West Indian Cricket test team. He has spent the last two years helping his father record his memoirs.

Endnotes

Foreword

1   *Lest We Forget*, page 137, published by Nottingham West Indian Combined Ex-Services Association, in association with Hansib Publishing (Caribbean) Ltd, 1966

2   *Lest We Forget* (1996), pages 141/142, published by Nottingham West Indian Combined Ex-Services Association, in association with Hansib Publishing (Caribbean) Ltd, 1966]

The British in Jamaica

1   *From Columbus to Castro, The History of the Caribbean, 1492-1969* By Eric Eustace Williams (12 Apr 1984)

2   (World Atlas, National Library of Jamaica, Digi Jamaica, and Britannia.)